JOVE

W9-ATV-055

ISBN 978-0-515-14472-7

9 780515 144727

5 0 5 9 9

S > EAN

355

LONGARM

AND THE
MYSTERIOUS MR. JIGGS

◆ TABOR EVANS ◆

ONE STORE, ONE SALOON, ONE CRAZY TOWN

Nobody's Fools

"Step aside, Harold. Me and James are gonna beat on this son of a bitch for a spell . . ."

"You'd best not do any such thing," the barber warned. "If you Wickets fuck up one more time, you'll be banned."

"Is this his coat over here? It is, ain't it?" James asked. He sidled over beside Longarm's coat and gunbelt. He was grinning when he slid Longarm's double-action .45 Colt from its holster. He turned to face Longarm.

"Not so tough now, are you?" George taunted.

"Maybe we'll just shoot your ass and take what we want off your dead body, *Mr.* London." James's sneer made the word *mister* sound like a curse word.

"No!" George quickly barked. "He said . . . I mean . . . you shouldn't ought to do that."

"Who said?" Longarm asked.

"Nobody," George answered.

"I won't take easy to the thought of bein' shot," Longarm warned. "An', if I have t' shoot, I won't waste no time trying t' just wound you, James. I'll drill you right in the belly. Now I've warned you fair and square so get the hell out o' here."

James Wicket looked down at the Colt revolver in his hand, then used both thumbs to draw the hammer back to firing position.

Longarm's .41-caliber derringer roared, the muzzle flash from it setting the barber's sheet on fire . . .

TABOR EVANS

LONGARM

AND THE MYSTERIOUS MR. JIGGS

JOVE BOOKS, NEW YORK

THE BERKLEY PUBLISHING GROUP
Published by the Penguin Group
Penguin Group (USA) Inc.
375 Hudson Street, New York, New York 10014, USA
Penguin Group (Canada), 90 Eglinton Avenue East, Suite 700, Toronto, Ontario M4P 2Y3, Canada
(a division of Pearson Penguin Canada Inc.)
Penguin Books Ltd., 80 Strand, London WC2R 0RL, England
Penguin Group Ireland, 25 St. Stephen's Green, Dublin 2, Ireland (a division of Penguin Books Ltd.)
Penguin Group (Australia), 250 Camberwell Road, Camberwell, Victoria 3124, Australia
(a division of Pearson Australia Group Pty. Ltd.)
Penguin Books India Pvt. Ltd., 11 Community Centre, Panchsheel Park, New Delhi—110 017, India
Penguin Group (NZ), 67 Apollo Drive, Rosedale, North Shore 0632, New Zealand
(a division of Pearson New Zealand Ltd.)
Penguin Books (South Africa) (Pty.) Ltd., 24 Sturdee Avenue, Rosebank, Johannesburg 2196,
South Africa

Penguin Books Ltd., Registered Offices: 80 Strand, London WC2R 0RL, England

This is a work of fiction. Names, characters, places, and incidents either are the product of the author's imagination or are used fictitiously, and any resemblance to actual persons, living or dead, business establishments, events, or locales is entirely coincidental.

LONGARM AND THE MYSTERIOUS MR. JIGGS

A Jove Book / published by arrangement with the author

PRINTING HISTORY
Jove edition / June 2008

ISBN: 978-0-515-14472-7

JOVE®
Jove Books are published by The Berkley Publishing Group,
a division of Penguin Group (USA) Inc.,
375 Hudson Street, New York, New York 10014.
JOVE is a registered trademark of Penguin Group (USA) Inc.
The "J" design is a trademark belonging to Penguin Group (USA) Inc.

PRINTED IN THE UNITED STATES OF AMERICA

10   9   8   7   6   5   4   3   2   1

Chapter 1

The cell door shut with a cold, metallic clang, and Custis Long breathed a sigh of relief for the first time in . . . he had to think back, which was difficult thanks to the fuzz in his brain . . . more than fifty hours.

Going without sleep was bad enough, but he was used to that. Being under constant tension was what had so thoroughly sapped his strength.

"Are you ready to sign for the sons o' bitches?" he asked Leon County Sheriff Bernard Cole.

"If I had my way, you'd of shot every last one of 'em between here and Denver. Shot trying to escape."

"Don't think they didn't want to," the tall deputy U.S. marshal said. His gaze shifted to the four men he had just delivered for trial and, likely, for hanging afterward. He glared at them, one by one. Scum. No more than that. Scum on the face of the earth. Rapists. There was nothing on God's green earth that he hated worse than a rapist. And these bastards the worst of all. The girl they attacked and kept captive for more than a week, sharing her back and forth between them, had been little more than a child. Their plan had been to kill and bury her when they were

1

done with her. Lucky for her—and for society at large—a posse of federal and local deputies got there first. The girl lived to testify against her attackers.

Now they faced trial. Before a territorial judge who could impose the death penalty if they were convicted and if he saw fit to do so. The deputy known as Longarm damn sure hoped His Honor saw fit.

"You look tired, Longarm," Sheriff Cole commented.

"Only because I am. Worn to a damn frazzle. What I want now is a bed. I'm gonna sleep straight through until tomorrow afternoon when that southbound coach leaves. And pity the poor son of a bitch that wakes me before then."

Longarm turned and left the cell block, a tall man, lean and craggy in a brown tweed coat, calfskin vest, and dark brown corduroy trousers over tall, black cavalry-style boots. He wore a double-action Colt revolver in a cross-draw rig and a flat-crowned brown Stetson. His shoulders were wide. At the moment, they were sagging with fatigue.

His handlebar mustache drooped, too. The ends needed waxing, and he was badly in need of a shave as well.

That would have to wait until he got back to Denver, where U.S. Marshal and former Texas Ranger William Vail had more work for his best deputy.

Longarm eased himself down onto a chair in the outer office and rubbed his eyes.

"I have those papers somewhere. Never mind. I'll write you out a receipt for them." Cole shook his head. "I don't know what the world is coming to, Longarm. They got forms for this and forms for that. Forms for every damn thing."

"Ain't that the truth. Billy Vail says he spends ninety percent of his time filling out paperwork, and I suspect he ain't real far off."

"Wait a minute. Here! I found them. All filled out by our

2

court clerk. Let me sign this and give you your copy to take back to Marshal Vail. How is he anyway?"

"Billy never changes."

"You say you're going back tomorrow?"

Longarm nodded and reached inside his coat for a pair of cheroots. He offered one to Cole, then bit the twist off the end of the other. He looked around the office, but did not see an ashtray or a cuspidor, so he spat the twist of tobacco into his palm and leaned forward to the match that Sheriff Cole scratched into flame and held for him. "Thanks. Yeah, I got to get back right away. Billy has something for me. Don't know exactly what yet, but he said I wasn't to dawdle." Longarm smiled. "O' course, that could just be his way o' keepin' me out of the bedrooms of any stray women I might run across."

Damn, those skinny little cheroots did taste good. Longarm drew the smoke in deep and savored it for a moment, then blew it out in a slow, white stream. He blew smoke rings with the last of it, then inhaled the excellent tobacco smoke again.

"I kind of thought you'd be going over to Yesterday to see Jim Franklin. He's town marshal there now, you know."

Longarm smiled. "Yeah, I do know, and I wish t' hell I could get over to see Jim. He's an old friend."

"That's what he said. To tell you the truth, I wondered if he was just blowing smoke up my ass, bragging about being friends with you and all."

"Sheriff, if Jim Franklin tells you something, you can turn right around and take it to the bank because it's damn sure golden. And yeah. He's a friend. A good friend. Used to be a helluva lawman, too. Back when I was learning the trade, Jim taught me much o' what I know. You can bank that, too."

Longarm collected the prisoner receipts that officially relieved Billy Vail of responsibility for the four men, then stood and stretched, yawning. "If you'll excuse me, Sheriff, I got t' go find a place I can crawl into for the night."

"Of course. Thanks for your help." Cole smiled. "Normally, I would offer you to sleep free in my cells, but I suspect you've seen enough of those boys."

"No, sir, I appreciate it, but I'm mighty happy to be shut of those sons of bitches. I might come back to see them hang, but that's the only thing more I'd want of them."

"All right then, Deputy. Have a good trip back to Denver."

The two men shook hands; then Longarm strode out into the slanting afternoon sunlight. He was bone-weary, but satisfied with the job he had done getting the prisoners here alive and in time for the trial.

Now his thoughts were on Denver and the job Billy had waiting for him there.

Chapter 2

The hansom cab pulled to a halt in front of the stone steps leading up to the Federal Building on Denver's Colfax Avenue. The sun had already disappeared behind the wall of craggy mountains to the west, and the city was in shadow. A city lamplighter was busy making his rounds along the major streets.

The cab door swung open and Longarm stepped out. He was clean-shaven and well rested.

"That will be twenty cents, sir," the driver called down from his perch high above the front wheels.

"Wait here a minute while I make sure I can still get in the building at this hour. I'll be right back."

"But sir—"

"Don't worry. I ain't running off. You still got my bag there." Longarm ran up the steps, checked to see that the door was not yet locked, then ran back down to the cab and reached inside for his old and somewhat battered carpetbag. "Twenty cents, you say."

"If it wouldn't be too much trouble," the driver said, his voice heavy with sarcasm.

"No trouble at all." Longarm dropped back in his pocket

the quarter he had intended to give the man, and carefully selected a pair of dimes instead. He handed those up to the impatient fellow and tipped his hat by way of a good-bye.

He picked up his bag and again mounted the long-familiar stone steps.

Only one lamp seemed to be burning inside the Federal Building, and it was seeping through the frosted glass to the outer office of the United States Marshal, First District Court of Colorado. Which was what the gilded lettering on that glass proclaimed.

Longarm opened that door and stepped inside. He smiled.

"I might of known it'd be you who's working late," he said to Billy Vail's faithful clerk, Henry. Henry had the appearance of a meek and mousy little man, but once he got his dander up, he was hell on wheels.

"Long," Henry said by way of a greeting. "You're late."

"Look, I know it's late an' the office is closed, but—"

"That isn't what I meant. You are two days late."

"The stagecoach broke an axle up above McConnellville someplace. That made me miss my connection in Jessup City, an' I sat on my butt there for two days before another southbound came through."

"You could have sent a wire. They do have telegraph service in Jessup City, don't they?"

Longarm grinned. "Likely they do. But maybe it wasn't exactly my butt I was settin' on. An' mayhap I was too busy t' think about sending any wires. Sorry."

"You don't look very sorry."

Longarm's grin got wider, but he did not elaborate any further on his unintended stopover.

"Do you happen to remember what day of the week this is?" Henry asked.

"Nope," Longarm said cheerfully. "I've kinda lost track. Is it important?"

"It was to Billy. He's already sent someone else to do the job he wanted you to take.

"You're incorrigible," Henry mumbled.

"Was that a compliment? You know how it flusters me when you use big words like that."

Henry wadded up a sheet of foolscap and threw it at Longarm, who ducked wildly to escape the harmless ball of paper. This from a man who could stand without flinching in the face of hostile gunfire.

"Anyway," Henry said, "it's Friday evening and Billy has gone for the weekend. I'm only here because I wanted some peace and quiet while I finish these reports."

"You mean I'm off for the weekend? No warrants to serve nor prisoners t' transport? None o' that good shit that they overpay me t' do?"

"No, you're free as a loon until Monday morning. And while we are on the subject of loons, may I suggest that you are indeed somewhat loony?"

"Hell, Henry, I like you, too. But say, why don't you an' me go have us a few drinks. Take in the show over at the Ophelia. I hear there's a new revue starting there."

"You would know about that sort of thing."

"If you're nice, I'll even let you buy a round," Longarm said. "Or two."

"You are certainly nice to me, aren't you. Well, then, put your bag down someplace where people won't trip over it. You don't want to have to drag that around at the same time you're having to carry me home."

"Why would I want t' take you home with me, Henry?" Longarm said with mock innocence.

"Idiot!" Henry wadded another ball of paper and threw

it, this time hitting Longarm in the chest. He stood and buttoned his vest. "Come on then. But you buy the first round."

"You're on," Longarm said, dropping his carpetbag on a chair and heading for the door.

Chapter 3

The little brunette slipped her arm through Longarm's and
smiled up at him from her five feet or so of height. The top
of her head barely came level with his shoulder. Little as
she was, though, she had tits enough for two women.
Deputy United States Marshal Custis Long had been known
to admire a tit or two in his time. Even ones that were more
than a mouthful.

"Did I hear somebody say that you're a genuine U.S.
marshal?" she purred.

"Only a deputy," Longarm said modestly.

"Do you have a big gun?"

He smiled down at the girl. Woman, he amended. She
was small and she still played the ingenue on stage, but
she'd gone past "girl" years back. Skillful makeup and a
well-practiced smile hid that fact from a distance, but up
close she quickly gained a dozen years or more.

She was cute, though. She damn sure was.

"I don't," he said, "think you're talkin' about this .45
Colt, which you can plainly see. But if you happen t' be
talking about my middle leg down here, well, you'd have t'
judge for yourself if it's big enough to suit your taste."

"Taste, you say?" The girl batted her eyes.

Henry, standing beside them, rolled his and shook his head. He leaned close to Longarm and said, "I think it's time for me to go home."

Longarm nodded without really paying attention. His focus was on the brunette.

"What'd you say your name is, honey?"

"My stage name is Collette. You can call me that if you like, but my real name is Abigail."

"It's a pleasure t' meet you, Abby. Tell me, though. Would you like t' go someplace quieter to talk?" The lobby of the mostly empty theater was quiet as a tomb.

"It is rather loud in here, isn't it. Just a minute. I'll fetch my shawl."

She was back in less than a minute, smiling and ready. Looking at those tits trying to escape from her dress made Longarm more than ready, too. "Let's go, darlin'."

"Do you have a place?" she asked.

He shook his head.

"Then follow me. Our troupe is staying at a boarding-house around the corner. It's close."

"I sure hope so," he said, which earned him an even brighter smile from Abby.

"I'll go in first," she said, "and go through and open the back door for you to slip inside. That way we won't be seen."

Longarm grinned. "I hope once we get upstairs we don't hafta worry about being heard."

Abby giggled and took him by the hand, practically running to get to her room.

Longarm ran his hands over the girl's back and down to her butt. He lightly squeezed one cheek and then the other. She was lying tight against his side with her face in his lap. He

10

could feel her tongue running around and around the head of his cock. Likely, he thought, Abigail could suck a hen's egg through a peashooter.

A soft, involuntary groan slipped out past his lips, and he had to make a conscious effort to keep from squirting into her mouth. Not that Abby probably would mind that, but he wanted to keep his edge until he could deposit that first broadside down where it rightly belonged.

"Don't. Ah, that's better. Yeah." He pulled her away and turned her onto her back, then took a handful of tit and squeezed, rolling her nipple between his thumb and middle finger.

"Oh, Oh! Ohhh!"

"Surely you didn't," he asked.

Abby nodded briskly. "I did, sweetie. Now touch me, please. Give the little man in the boat a ride."

Longarm chuckled and slipped two fingers into her. Abby was dripping wet, her flesh slippery and engorged. He found the little nubbin that guarded the entrance to her body, and played with it for a few moments. Abby's cries and arched back told him that she was a girl who was quick to climax and could do it over and over again.

"Yes, yes, sweetie." She pumped her hips, grinding herself against his knuckles and whimpering with pleasure.

Eventually, Abby collapsed back onto the bed. She was smiling.

"My turn," Longarm whispered.

Abby opened herself to him, and he slid full length into her. The girl's body was small, but she had no trouble accommodating all of him.

She was hot and slippery wet, and he held himself poised deep within her for a few heartbeats before he began the rhythmic pumping that brought so much pleasure.

11

"Nice," she said. "Yes. Hard now. I—I—I—" She never did quite finish what she was trying to say. Words turned to squeals and grunts of effort as she flung her belly hard against his.

Longarm felt the rising pressure in his balls. Rising beyond containment until he burst outward, spewing his juices.

He lay on top of her for long moments while he calmed his breathing. When he withdrew from her body, the air felt chilly on his wet cock.

"Here," she said. "Let me clean that for you." Smiling, Abby bent to him and once again took him into her mouth, cleansing his flesh of his juice and her own.

"Keep that up," he said, "and I'll be rolling you over onto your back again."

Abby laughed. And went back to sucking him harder than ever.

Sure enough. He was rolling her over in just another minute or two.

Chapter 4

"You look like shit," Henry said.

Longarm grinned. "Maybe so, but I had a helluva nice time getting this way."

"The little brunette?"

Longarm rolled his eyes, and Henry laughed, saying, "You know what they say about good things and small packages."

"Whoever says that knows what he's talking about," Longarm responded. He did not elaborate, but the truth was that just about the only sleep he got all weekend was when Abigail was away at the theater performing. She had performed in her bedroom, too, but there had been no one present to offer applause then.

"In case you're wondering," Henry said, "your bag is over here behind my desk. I didn't think it gave the proper impression to visitors over there where you left it Friday."

"Thanks. Not that there's all that much in it except dirty clothes and my supply of smokes." He yawned and rubbed his eyes.

"You haven't been home yet?" Henry asked.

13

Longarm shook his head. "No. I would of gone there this morning, except I didn't want Billy getting any madder at me than he already is."

"Then you're in luck. Billy was in the office sometime over the weekend. He left a note for me saying he has to make a quick trip to Kansas City. Some sort of consultation. He didn't say what about, but he did say he'll be gone most of this week. Maybe longer."

"Good. In that case, Henry, I'm going home. I'll get cleaned up an' take my laundry to the Chinaman. Get a little sleep, too, I think. But I'll be in tomorrow morning for certain sure, an' if anything comes up . . ."

Henry nodded. "I know where to find you."

"Thanks, Henry. You're a pal." Longarm picked up his carpetbag and headed back outside to search for a cab. Normally, he walked to and from work, but this morning he was just too damned tired to go hiking. Better to let a horse do it.

His rented rooms, as close to being a home as he'd had in many years, smelled of naphtha soap and sunshine. Apparently, the hired girl had been in to change his sheets. She had tidied the place while she was at it.

Longarm dumped the contents of his carpetbag into a cloth sack ready to carry to the laundry, stacked his few remaining cheroots and two boxes of .45 cartridges on the tiny correspondence desk under his window, and shoved the now empty carpetbag into the wardrobe along with his saddle and hanging clothes. Then he quickly stripped down to his balbriggans. He was so tired, he did not intend even to clean his revolver. That chore could wait until he got a little sleep.

Finally, eagerly, he turned to the narrow, lumpy, wonderfully familiar refuge of his bed.

It was only then that he noticed the envelope placed carefully onto his pillow.

Damned if it wasn't correctly addressed to him, too. He had no idea who it could be from. This was the first piece of mail he had received here at home in . . . he could not remember how long it might have been. Months. Years? A long time certainly.

Longarm was accustomed to receiving telegraph messages and occasionally mail, but those items were related to his work and were delivered to the marshal's office in the Federal Building.

This looked like it was personal.

He fetched his pocketknife out of the dresser drawer where he had just put it and carefully slit the envelope open.

The message inside was brief. Longarm turned pale when he read it. Then his face darkened with fury.

He spun around and snatched his carpetbag out of the wardrobe, tore his dresser drawers open, and began hurriedly stuffing clothing into the bag. He added the cheroots and cartridges on top of the clothing, changed to fresh balbriggans, and quickly dressed, strapping his .45 in place last.

When he was ready to leave, he took his saddle and Winchester out of the wardrobe, picked them up along with the carpetbag, and let himself out into the hall.

His steps were quick as he thundered down the stairs and out into the street. He waved a hansom cab to him and threw his things into it almost before the driver brought the vehicle to a rocking halt.

"Union Depot," he called up to the driver. "Double fare if you hurry."

"Yes, *sir!*"

The young fellow on the driving box cracked his whip, and the hack took off with a lurch.

Chapter 5

Longarm stepped down onto the bare, sun-bleached planks of the Union Pacific loading platform, in Jessup City, and carried his gear across the broad street to the Hopkins Express Company office. He knew it well, having used it just a few days earlier.

"Why, good morning, Marshal." The clerk smiled. "Forget something, did you?"

"No. I have t' go north again. Yesterday."

"Even we can't get you there that quick, Marshal."

"I meant the town."

"Yesterday is the name of a town?"

"Yes, 'tis. Up near Buffalo."

"At least, that is a town I've heard of before. Up north, you say?" The clerk plucked his rate sheet from a shelf near his desk and pored over it. After a minute or so, he shook his head. "I'm sorry, Marshal. I don't see any town by that name here. Is it new?"

"Couple years, I think," Longarm said.

The clerk looked again. "You say it's near Buffalo? I can get you on the northbound to Buffalo, and you can hire a horse there or a carriage if you prefer."

"When is that stage scheduled?"

"Our northbound left about an hour ago. There will be another tomorrow morning at that same time."

"Damn!" Longarm mumbled. He had two choices, neither of them good. He could sit here twiddling his thumbs for almost twenty-four hours, or he could hire a horse and ride it half to death trying to get there. One horse and no relays along the way meant he would have to stop overnight to rest the animal. The question was, which would get him there the quickest in the long run?

It would be more satisfying, of course, to leap on a saddle horse and go hell-for-leather up the trail on his own.

But the simple truth was that waiting for the stage, with its relays of teams and running day and night, would likely get him there quicker. Dammit!

"Put me on that stage, friend."

"Do you want to leave the saddle and rifle here? I have a locked storage closet you can use. No charge, of course."

"Yeah, that'd be convenient. Thanks." Longarm handed over those bulky items, but kept his carpetbag with him. "Now, d'you know where I might find a clean bed until morning?"

"Of course. You just go . . ."

Longarm wanted to lie down and sleep more than just about anything, but there were matters that had to be tended to first. He left his carpetbag on the foot of the bed and let himself back out.

He went to Finneran's General Mercantile and bought a handful of cheroots that he stuffed into a coat pocket, then walked back to the Union Pacific station.

"Yes, sir?"

"I need to send a telegram."

"Of course. Our rate is . . ." The sight of Longarm's badge cut short the man's discussion of charges. "Yes, uh, just write down what you want me to send and where it should go."

Longarm addressed the message to Henry at the U.S. marshal's office in Denver.

CALLED AWAY FOR EMERGENCY STOP ASSISTING
LOCAL LAW ENFORCEMENT STOP BACK SOONEST
POSSIBLE END SIGNED LONG

"Thank you, friend. Now can you tell me, please, where I can get the best meal in town?"

"Sure thing. You go across the street here and down . . ."

The café was small, but it was doing a good trade, mostly men having their morning breaks hunched over coffee cups. Off to one side, three ladies were drinking coffee, too—out of much nicer cups than the men were given, Longarm noticed—and chattering softly among themselves.

"Coffee?" the young girl in a white apron offered.

"Please. An' a menu. I haven't had time t' eat lately."

She smiled. "No one should get that busy."

"I agree with you on that, miss, but it happens."

"We don't have an actual menu. Do you want breakfast or lunch?"

"How's about some of each. A nice steak. Fried eggs. Fried 'taters if you got some. And biscuits. D'you have good biscuits here?"

"My mother is famous for her biscuits. Ask anybody."

"Ah, I'd just as soon try them for myself."

"Anything else?"

"That will do me nicely, thank you."

19

The girl went away without bothering to write anything down. Not that it was a complicated order. Longarm leaned back, trying to will himself to relax. He had been on edge ever since he opened that letter. He needed to get past that. He needed to be able to think clearly now.

He pulled out a cheroot and lighted it, more because he wanted something to do with his hands than because he really wanted the smoke.

Tomorrow. He could not accomplish anything until that stage left come tomorrow morning.

Tomorrow. Then Yesterday.

Chapter 6

Longarm took the last bite of steak, a piece he had saved for last that was edged with yellowish and extra tasty fat. He leaned back in his chair. He felt much better with a good meal behind him.

"Would you like dessert now, sir?"

"No, thanks. I'm full clear t' the top." He smiled at the girl. She wasn't pretty, but she was an attentive waitress and very pleasant. He figured she'd earned a nice tip, and he intended to see that she had one.

"Raspberry cobbler baked fresh this morning," she said.

"Not even for your mama's cobbler," Longarm said. "But I could stand one more refill of the coffee." Rye whiskey would be even better, but he could take care of that desire as soon as he left the café. A whiskey. Then a shave. And maybe another whiskey before he went and tried out that bed. Lordy, but he was tired. Oh, and he needed a bottle of rye to carry with him in his carpetbag. He hadn't had a chance to replace the one he'd emptied on this last trip out.

The girl went into the back and emerged with a carafe of coffee. She was halfway to Longarm's table when one of the customers, a large man seated with two friends, grabbed her elbow, spinning her around.

"Here. Give me some of tha—*ouch*, damn you!" Some of the hot coffee spilled, splashing onto the fellow's arm and down his shirt. He jumped out of his chair. "You clumsy little bitch."

The man, who was a head taller and probably a hundred pounds heavier than the girl, reared back and slapped her. Hard, the back of his hand slashing across her face and spinning her half around. Blood began to flow out of the corner of her mouth and from her nose.

The girl burst into tears. She pulled the carafe back, and was quite obviously thinking about throwing the rest of that steaming-hot coffee onto the son of a bitch.

If she did that, Longarm figured there was a very good chance that the bastard would punch her in the face.

"Whoa there," Longarm said, rising and coming up behind her. He smiled down at her and gently removed the carafe from her grip, turned, and set the coffee down on the nearest table. "It's all right now. Go wash your face. Time you get back, this gentleman here is gonna apologize for acting like he done."

"Fuck you!" the "gentleman" in question roared.

The three ladies who had been having tea and pastry at a window table turned pale at the coarse language. They hurriedly gathered up their bonnets and scurried outside.

"Go on now," Longarm urged, smiling at the girl all the while. "He'll settle down in just a minute now."

"Fuck you!" the fellow snarled again.

"Larry, for crying out loud, will you sit down and shut up. Please. This gentleman is trying to help. Can't you see that?"

"Then fuck you, too, Thomas." Larry glared at his friend, still seated at the table, then swung to face Longarm.

Longarm edged the girl to one side and gave her a little nudge in the back to send her on her way. He waited until she was safely into the kitchen, then turned his smile on the fellow they called Larry.

"Larry, m' man, you got a lot to learn about how t' act in public. I can tell you've had nothing an' nobody but sheep for company for all these years, so you're t' be pitied instead o' looked down upon. Because o' that, Larry, I forgive you for being such a stupid asshole. I surely do." Longarm's smile was broad.

"Sheep. *Sheep?* Why, you . . ."

One of Larry's friends laughed out loud.

"I kill every sheep I see, and I just may decide to kill you, too, mister," Larry blustered.

"Careful what you say, old son. You don't wanta go an' make me mad."

Larry balled up his fists, lowered his head, and charged.

He ran into an obstacle that was every bit as solid as if he'd walked into a doorjamb. Longarm broke the man's nose with that first straight right hand. Blood flew and Larry's head snapped back. He staggered, caught his balance, and shook his head, causing bright red droplets to decorate pretty much everything and everyone nearby.

"Damn you!"

He tried again. This time, Longarm sidestepped the charge and met him with a hard, underhand punch, knuckles extended into the pit of his stomach. Larry doubled over, then, wheezing, managed to straighten up in time for Longarm to hit him again with a right-left-right-combination, jaw-belly-jaw.

Longarm looked at Larry's friends, who made no attempt to come to his rescue. "You boys do what you think is best," he said, "but I'd suggest you take this idiot off somewhere an' let him calm down before he gets hurt."

One of them sighed. "You're right, mister. Sorry. He can be a hothead sometimes."

"So I noticed. Take him on out then, please." He turned his attention to Larry. "What I'm gonna suggest is that next time you come to town you apologize to that nice little girl. She didn't deserve having t' take crap off the likes o' you."

Larry did not say anything. But he was listening. Longarm was sure about that. His chums got up, dropped more than enough money on the table to pay for their coffee and crullers, and hustled Larry out.

Longarm waited until the waitress peeked into the room. When she saw that it was safe, she came in carrying a freshly filled carafe.

"That's all right, miss. Don't waste that in my cup. Reckon I've had enough for right now. Thank you, though." He smiled at her. "Are you all right now?"

She nodded. There were tear tracks on her cheeks, but she had her breathing under control. She scrubbed at her eyes with the back of one wrist. "Are you sure you won't have more coffee?"

"I'm fine. Thanks."

Longarm figured his meal was worth twenty-five cents. He left fifty.

He was not ten feet out the door before he heard the deadly *cla-clack* of a pistol being cocked behind him.

Chapter 7

Longarm spun around, dropping into a crouch at the same time. His Colt flashed in his hand, the hammer coming back even before he identified his target.

It was Larry, who held a large-caliber revolver. Larry's pistol roared, flame and smoke gushing from the muzzle.

Longarm could feel the impact of the sound like a blow on his cheeks and eyes, but the bullet flew over his head.

His own slug flew true, however, ripping out Larry's throat. Blood sprayed onto both of Larry's horrified friends as their companion toppled facedown onto the boards of the sidewalk.

Longarm rose from his crouch, revolver still leveled. "Are you boys in or out o' this thing?"

One of them, the one who had tried to be the peacemaker inside the café, looked like he might make a try at avenging his friend. A long look into the barrel of Longarm's Colt dissuaded him.

The other one stammered, "He-he only wanted to scare you, mister. He only wanted to b-blow one over your head and put a fright in you."

Longarm grunted, "Then he shoulda hung a sign around his neck or something."

"Mister, is he dead? Did you k-kill him?"

"Well, if I didn't, I'll have to shoot the sonuvabitch again." Longarm glared at the two cowhands who were upright, and at the one that was lying there with the last of his blood draining down between the boards. "Are you boys in this thing or out?"

"Me? Oh, no. Not me, mister," one of them said.

"You?" Longarm prompted the other one, emphasizing the question with a wave of the Colt that he still had in his hand.

"N-no, sir."

Longarm heard footsteps behind him and an authoritative "What's going on here?"

He only half-turned around so that he could keep an eye on the dead man's friends. The man coming up behind was carrying a sawed-off shotgun and wore a badge on his chest.

"Drop your gun, mister."

Longarm complied. Sort of. He shoved his Colt back into the leather. But he still kept one eye on the cowboys. "This man drew on me. Behind my back, I might add."

"He only wanted to scare this dude, Andy. I swear. Just wanted to scare him."

"But he did draw?"

"Yes, sir."

"I heard two shots. Who fired first?"

"Larry did, Marshal. But he just wanted to . . ."

"I heard you the first time, Thomas." The town marshal shook his head and peered down at the dead man. "Just how did he think this fella was supposed to know it was only in fun? Did he ever think about that? Dumb son of a bitch never thought about much of anything, did he."

The marshal turned his attention to Longarm, who had taken his Colt out again and was engaged in reloading the chamber he had emptied into Larry.

"You'll have to stay in town here until we've held an inquest, mister. Not much doubt which way they'll find, but you'll have to stay anyway."

"I don't think so," Longarm said. He snapped the loading gate closed and pushed the revolver back into his holster.

The town marshal reached for the small of the stock on his shotgun, his thumbs lying over the twin hammers. "What did you say, fella?"

Longarm reached inside his coat and brought his wallet out. He flipped it open to display his badge. "My name is Long, Marshal. Deputy U.S. marshal under Billy Vail down in Denver. I'm sorry, but I don't have time to fuck around waiting here for a death inquest. I'll be glad to give you a sworn statement about this, but I'm leaving on the northbound coach first thing tomorrow morning, with or without your permission."

"Long. You're the one they call Longarm?"

"That I am, sir."

The muzzles of the shotgun pointed down toward the ground, and the town marshal began to grin. "I'll be damned. Longarm. Right here in my own town." He looked at Larry's friends and growled, "You fellas tote Larry over to the barbershop. Mind you go around to the back door, though. Don't be dragging a corpse in through the front. It might put folks off. You, sir," he said to Longarm, "please come with me. We'll go to my office and you can write out your statement. I won't take much of your time, I promise."

"Fair enough, Marshal," Longarm said. "You lead. I'll follow."

27

He had briefly forgotten how very tired he was. Now it came crushing back on him. Right now, he wanted nothing so much as that bed.

Soon. Soon.

Chapter 8

Longarm was at the express company office a half hour early, feeling better after a good night's sleep and with a hot breakfast in his belly. He had needed both. He collected his saddle and rifle from the friendly station manager and took them outside. He set his gear down on the sidewalk and slouched against the wall.

Others, presumably other passengers waiting for the same stage, drifted in over the next twenty minutes or so. A Concord could hold a dozen people. Not comfortably perhaps, but it could hold them. As it happened, only nine people showed up counting Longarm himself. There were two women, one fairly nice-looking, and a young boy included.

The passengers arrived. The coach did not.

One of the passengers, a fellow who looked uncomfortable in a no-longer-fashionable coat and foulard tie, began to nip at a bottle and to loudly complain to no one in particular. It would be nice, Longarm thought, if that particular gentleman—he used the term loosely—were to miss the coach.

A half hour after they were supposed to depart, the

stagecoach wheeled in, the horses sweating and dripping foam at their muzzles. Whatever it was that delayed them, the coach hadn't been late for lack of trying.

The jehu and the helper coming off the southbound leg quickly unloaded the luggage and rooftop freight, while the northbound crew and two stable hands broke down the hitch. The stable hands took all six horses away to walk them until they cooled. Then the fresh crew began quickly building the new six-up with fresh animals already harnessed and ready to go into the traces.

It took less than ten minutes to get the fresh team in place, and a few more to load the passengers' luggage. Longarm's carpetbag went into the cavernous boot on the back of the big coach. His saddle and scabbarded Winchester went up top along with two other saddles and several crates of northbound freight.

The gent with the bottle complained constantly while the work was going on. Longarm thought the crews did an admirable job in the changeover. This fellow obviously did not.

The final straw was when the asshole sidled up to the younger and prettier of the two women and very loudly proclaimed, "Li'l lady, you don' worry about nothin'. You set wid me. I watch out for you."

The young woman turned pale. "Sir, I am a married woman. Please keep your distance."

"Li'l lady, you don' worry 'bout nothin'. I mean that. Nothin'."

Longarm stepped up beside the man and whispered, "Psst! Sit with me, friend. I got me a bottle, too. Bigger'n that one in your pocket."

"Yeah?"

"Really," Longarm said. It was not a lie. Not exactly. He did have a bottle. In his luggage.

The gent smiled.

"What say we have a taste of yours before we get in the coach," Longarm suggested.

"Sure. You bet, mister."

Longarm held out his hand and the gent grabbed his bottle out of his coat pocket.

"Oh, jeez," Longarm grumbled as the pint bottle somehow slipped from his fingers and broke on the rocky soil at their feet. "I sure am sorry, friend. But don't worry. Let's get in the coach. You and me will sit together."

They waited for the two women and the boy to get in first. The ladies did not seem to know each other, but they sat together as if for both company and protection. The two sat on the forward-facing bench at the back of the Concord. The boy chose a rear-facing window seat in the middle. Longarm guided his new "friend" onto the rear-facing bench at the front of the coach, as far away from the ladies as he could get.

As soon as all the passengers were aboard, the jehu called down, "Rolling out, folks. Here we go."

They heard the crack of a whip and felt the rocking lurch as the big coach rumbled into motion.

"Psst." The gent with the thirst nudged Longarm in the ribs. "Lemme see that bottle, will ya."

Longarm smiled and leaned close to the fellow's ear. Very slowly and distinctly he said, "Shut your fucking mouth and keep it shut or I'm gonna start breaking your bones. One by one by one. And I am gonna enjoy every one that busts."

"You can't . . ." The fellow's sputtering fury stopped when he looked into the steel of Longarm's eyes.

"Not . . . one . . . fucking . . . word. You got me, mister? Not one." Longarm's knuckles pressed painfully hard into the man's short ribs, down between them where it could not be seen by the other passengers.

The fellow winced and turned pale. "Y-yes, sir."

Longarm smiled at him. "Thank you," he said just as pleasantly as he knew how. "Now let's us set back an' enjoy the ride. Might as well. We're gonna be together for the next couple days."

The man groaned. But he did not object.

Chapter 9

The jehu climbed down off the driving box, came around, and opened the passenger door. He stuck his head in and said, "Time for your supper break, folks. You have half an hour to refresh yourselves."

The man pulled a step stool out from under the coach and set it down so the ladies would have an easier exit. Then he hurried forward to help his assistant and a man from the relay station make the changeover to another team for the next long pull.

They had been on the road ten hours, and the sources of shallow conversation with total strangers had long since dried up. Most of the passengers were either sleeping or pretending to. The badly dressed fellow with the big thirst was slumped over with his head on Longarm's shoulder. His mouth was open, and he was drooling onto his tie.

Longarm elbowed the man in the side. "Wake up, neighbor. Time for supper." He leaned close to the man's ear and in a quieter voice added, "But if you buy another bottle while we're here, I'm gonna bust it over your head." He smiled nicely. None of the other passengers could have guessed his message, at least not by Longarm's facial expression.

They might have gotten an inkling from the posture of the other fellow, however. He sat rigidly upright, unsmiling and shrinking as far away into the corner of the bench as he could get.

The stationmaster helped the ladies down and announced, "The outhouses are around the corner there. There's wash-basins and soap laid ready. No charge for those. Fresh tow-els is five cents each, or you can use whatever is already there. Supper is stew and soda bread. Twenty-five cents for that with coffee thrown in free. Five cents for the coffee if you don't wanta eat. Come on in now. Come on in."

Longarm held back until everyone else was off the coach. His seatmate stayed where he was, too. But then he had no choice. Longarm was blocking him in.

"Remember what I told you," Longarm said when the others had climbed out of the coach and gone inside. "Bring another bottle onto this coach, an' I'll break it an' the hand that holds it. Do we understand each other?"

"If I had a gun . . ."

Longarm snorted. "If you had a gun, you wouldn't be ballsy enough to use it anyway. An' if you did try me, it wouldn't bother me even a little bit to see t' your burying. Go on now. Get outa here."

The passenger left the coach and Longarm followed. He went around to the outhouses and took a piss, then washed up before going inside thinking to try the stew. When he got there, his thirsty seatmate was off to one side buying a quart bottle. Longarm doubted the bottle held milk. He meant what he had said, though.

The other male passengers were occupying one end of the long table, leaving the other end for the ladies and boy.

Longarm had little choice but to sit near the women. Not that he minded.

He removed his Stetson and nodded to the ladies. "Mind if I join you folks?"

"Please do," the older woman said. "Move over, Ty. Give the gentleman room."

The boy dutifully shifted a quarter inch or so to one side. He was busy eyeing the butt of Longarm's Colt.

A serving woman in a crisply fresh apron came by and exchanged a tin bowl and china mug for Longarm's quarter. The stew, bread, and coffee were already set out on the table for diners to help themselves. All three were hot and reasonably tasty. Longarm was glad to get them after a full day spent inside that stagecoach.

He barely had time to finish his meal and step outside to light a cheroot before the jehu was calling, "Time to load up, folks. We'll be pulling out quick as we get this new team hooked up."

The assistant driver and station helper were already leading the new horses into place.

Longarm held back, enjoying his smoke as long as he could before boarding. The gent with the bottle remained indoors where he could drink without having his fingers broken. He was still there ten minutes later when the driver cracked his whip and the coach jerked into motion.

Some hours later, rolling through the night with most of the passengers asleep, the young woman on the back bench came forward. She leaned close to Longarm and said, "Thank you, sir. You are very gallant."

"*De nada,*" he mumbled. "It was nothin.'"

"To me it was."

"That's fine then."

"May I tell you something?" She laid her fingertips

lightly on his wrist. He could not see her in the dark, but there was something in his voice that suggested she was smiling.

"Anything," he said.

"Back there. When I told that man that I am married?"

"Yes, ma'am, I remember that."

She leaned even closer. "I lied."

Then, giggling, she was gone, fleeing back to her own seat in the rear of the coach.

Longarm was sorely disappointed the next day when he left the coach at Hancock's relay station, the closest the route came to the young town of Yesterday. Disappointed because the young lady—she had grown more and more attractive to him as the miles rolled out behind them—was continuing on to Buffalo.

Longarm tipped his hat in a silent good-bye, and immediately put her out of mind while he found the stationmaster to see about hiring a horse.

Chapter 10

The town of Yesterday was in the foothills of the Big Horn range south of Buffalo, Wyoming. Longarm had never been there, and knew of it only because of his friend and mentor Jim Franklin.

According to what he was told by Leon County Sheriff Bernard Cole, Yesterday got its start as a placer digging. Someone hauled in several wagonloads of goods and started a store to service the needs of the miners. When the gold played out, the store remained.

Cowhands and sheepherders working the grasslands to the east came to the store, as did prospectors, shoestring miners, and trappers coming down out of the mountains to the west.

Men like that wanted refreshment when they took a break from their labors, so soon a saloon was built close to the store.

The men wanted more than liquor when they were getting that refreshment, so a small brothel was created to meet their needs.

All of those establishments required people to run them,

so houses were built and a boardinghouse opened for the residents, as well as a hotel for the transients.

Lumber was needed to build those structures. Someone brought in the equipment to erect a small sawmill. Timber was needed to feed the mill, so loggers came in.

Livestock had to be quartered while people were visiting the growing community, so a livery stable was built to fill that need.

Both humans and animals had to be fed while they were there, so a grocery, a butcher shop, and a feed and grain business came in.

One thing led to another and despite its isolation, before anyone hardly noticed, a town had come into existence.

Placer diggings came and went. This one gave the impression that it was going to stay.

It was late in the day when Longarm got his first look at Yesterday. The town was nestled at the bottom of one of the folds in the earth that flanked the Big Horns. The sun had long since disappeared behind the rugged mountains even though it was still an hour or more from sunset.

He would have gotten there earlier, but back at the express company relay station he was unable to hire a horse that was trained to accept a saddle and rider. He had to make do with what was available, that being a small mare and a light buggy.

A saddle horse would definitely have been his preference. A buggy is restricted to the roads. A saddle horse can move freely, independent of roads.

Still, the driving rig got him to Yesterday. That was the important thing.

"Where can I find a room for the night?" Longarm asked the fellow at the livery. The man had one leg shorter than the other and a shoulder that did not move properly. Longarm guessed he was an old cowhand who had busted one too many bad horses and gotten busted up himself. Now he was tending animals he could no longer ride.

"The hotel is that place there. There's no sign but no need for one. The folks who come around here already know about it. If they don't, they soon enough learn. Just like you already did. Want a word of advice, mister?"

"Sure."

"Pay the extra for a room all by yourself. Some of the boys that come around here get real rowdy. If you know what I mean."

Longarm chuckled. "I b'lieve I do, friend, and I thank you."

"You want grain for this here mare? Grain costs ten cents a day extra."

Longarm thought about it for a moment, then shook his head. "I won't be using her hard. Might not be using her at all for a little while. She don't need graining if you got decent hay."

"It's good grass hay, no mold or anything."

"Then she won't need grain, I think."

"Give me a hand, mister," the liveryman said. "Quick as I get this harness off, we'll roll your buggy over behind the shed there. Mind if I ask you something?"

"Go ahead."

"You in town on business?"

"You could say that."

"Then if you want some advice," he smiled, "free for nothing and worth every penny you pay for it, what I'd say is that you stop by the saloon there. Ask for Mr. Jiggs. Introduce yourself. Just sort of say hello and you want to get acquainted. He'll let you know the way things are here."

"The way things . . . I don't rightly get what you mean, neighbor."

"What I mean is that you don't want to be conducting any business in Yesterday without you first speak with Mr. Jiggs. You'll understand what I'm saying after you meet him."

"Now you have me curious. But I reckon I will do what you say. I'll go by and meet Mr. Jiggs before I talk business with anybody."

"You'll be glad you did." The liveryman draped the mare's harness over some pegs on the wall, then picked up the buggy's poles. "Give a shove here, mister. We'll roll this outfit out of the way. Then you can go get your room at the hotel yonder."

"Thanks." Longarm helped the fellow push the buggy away, then picked up his carpetbag and rifle. He left his saddle in the back of the buggy. There did not seem any point in dragging it along with him to the hotel.

On his way over to the hotel, it occurred to him that no one in Yesterday knew him. No one here knew that he carried a badge.

Perhaps, just perhaps, that was a good thing.

And perhaps it should stay that way for the time being.

Chapter 11

"Two bits," the desk clerk said, "and you share the bed."

"How much for a room all to myself?" Longarm asked.

"That'd be four bits."

"That suits me."

"In advance."

Longarm dug into his pocket and paid. He would not have felt right about putting the charges on an expense voucher, even if he had not decided to remain anonymous for the time being. After all, he had not been sent here by Billy Vail. This trip was strictly on his own.

The clerk reached under the counter and brought out a guest register. He flipped it open and spun it around to face Longarm. "Your name, sir?"

"Uh . . . Curtis," Longarm said. "Curtis London."

"Sign here, Mr. London." The man uncorked the inkwell on the counter and handed Longarm a pen, then laid a key on the counter. "Your room is through this door and down the hall. It's the last one on the left. I hope you enjoy your stay in Yesterday."

"Thanks." Longarm carried his gear to the room, which was spartan but seemed clean enough. At least, the sheets were reasonably fresh and there was a down-filled pillow on the bed. The bed consisted of a crude frame laced with a web of ropes. A hay-filled mattress ticking lay on top of the webbing.

There was a window overlooking a trash-strewn alley beside the hotel. A few threads caught on some roofing nails above the window suggested there might have been a curtain in place at some point, but it was gone now.

There was no washbasin, no mirror, no chest of drawers or wardrobe. There was a thunder mug—but no lid for it—under the bed.

Spartan indeed.

But it would do.

Longarm shoved his carpetbag under the bed and covered the Winchester with a blanket. Not that he expected that would accomplish anything if a thief came to call when he was out, but at least it would keep the weapon out of plain sight if someone happened to look in, which would be easily done by anyone who wanted to. The key was a simple skeleton key; the lock could be readily picked by anyone who cared to come inside.

"I need two things," Longarm told the desk clerk when he returned to the hotel lobby. "I need an outhouse and a place t' have supper."

"The shitter is out back. There's a wash shed out there, too. The door is just past your room there. As for supper, there's a café two doors down. Best restaurant in town. Only one, too."

Longarm thanked the man and found his way to the outhouse. He took care of business there, then washed and brushed the dust of travel from his clothing as best he could. He took the alley past his room window to get back to the street, and found the café the desk clerk told him about.

By then, it was nearly dark. Lights glowed through windows up and down the street. Yesterday had no such amenities as street lamps. Nearly all the businesses in town were closing down at this hour, and men were on the street heading to their homes for the evening.

An exception was the saloon where the hostler said he could find Mr. Jiggs. Its windows were ablaze with light.

Longarm's stomach suggested that supper come before either Mr. Jiggs or a beverage, so he headed into the café. He was lucky to find an empty seat. The place was nearly full, and more men were on their way.

It was run by a fat Mexican in a filthy apron. The man had mustaches that would put Longarm's to shame. They were shiny black, waxed, and perfectly curled. Longarm would have guessed them to extend a foot to each side had the curls been pulled out straight.

He looked for a menu posted on the wall, but did not see one.

"How do I know what you have?" he asked.

"You don't," the Mexican told him. "I cook one thing at a time. The choice you got is to eat it or don't. You wanta eat, mister?"

Longarm looked at the plates already on the two long tables. It looked like son-of-a-bitch stew served with hot bread, soft cheese, and coffee. The smell of it had his nostrils quivering and his mouth watering. "I'll eat."

"Two bits. In advance."

Longarm paid, and took the bowl and large spoon that he was handed.

"I ain't seen you in town before," offered the man sitting to his left.

"Just got here this afternoon. What's it like here?"

"I been in worse places."

43

"Much trouble here?"

"Not so much," the gent said.

Damn, that stew was good. And the bread. There was no butter, but the diners were spreading the soft white cheese on their bread instead. Longarm tried it. It was a little strong—goat cheese most likely—but very tasty. "Pass me some more of that bread, would you? Thanks."

"So what do you do, mister? What brings you to Yesterday?"

"I'm a broker," Longarm told him.

"Do you mean you're broke? Don't have no money?"

"No, I'm a commodities broker. I buy and sell, or arrange for someone to buy and sell, all sorts of things. I'm thinking maybe t' pick up some business here."

It was a question he had known would be coming somewhere along the way, and one he had been giving some thought to ever since he left the livery. It was an answer that would cover a multitude of sins since a broker can be anything. Or nothing.

"Lemme have that bread back, would you?"

Longarm returned the rapidly emptying breadbasket, and hoped someone would be along soon to refill it.

"Could I have some more o' that cheese, please?"

Chapter 12

The saloon, apparently the only one in town, was nicer than he would have expected in such an isolated community. Ornate chandeliers spread light over the gaming tables. Those included simple card tables, a wheel of fortune, a faro setup, and roulette.

Flocked wallpaper and mirrors in gilded frames covered the walls, the mirrors making the large room seem even larger than it was.

A bar ran along the full length of one side wall. The cuspidors and foot rail were highly polished brass. The shelves on the wall behind the bar held what must have been more than a hundred bottles, and the beer was being drawn from a source that was either hidden beneath the bar surface, or perhaps was stored in a basement beneath the building.

It was a saloon that would fit in comfortably in Denver or Kansas City or even in San Francisco.

The place was not what he would call crowded, but it was certainly doing a good business.

Longarm crossed the floor to the bar and got a prompt welcome from the gent in the clean, white apron. "What'll it be, friend?"

"I'll have a beer, please. An' for future reference, d'you have Maryland distilled rye on hand?"

"I have three brands of rye whiskey. Two of 'em come out of Maryland. Would you like one now? On the house since this seems to be your first visit."

"Why, that's mighty nice o' you." Longarm smiled. "Can't pass up a free whiskey, now can I?"

"Still want that beer to go with it?" the bartender asked.

"Sure. And I thank you."

The barman drew Longarm's beer, then rummaged along the shelf of bottles until he found the two he wanted. He carried them back to show the labels to Longarm. "How about these?"

"My friend, you've just made me a happy fellow. I'd like a little from that bottle in your left hand."

"Done," the bartender said. "Next time you come in, I'll know what your preference is."

"Thank you."

"My name is Pete, by the way," the bartender said.

"I'm Curtis London." He'd almost forgotten what name he was traveling under. Longarm laid a nickel down to pay for the beer—only the whiskey had been offered for free— and lifted the rye. Rather than drinking immediately, he smelled of it, the aroma rich and earthy from the grain it came from. He tasted it and let it lie on his tongue for a moment. Marvelous.

Pete was down at the other end of the long bar talking with someone there.

Longarm savored the rye for a moment, then tried the beer. The flavor was crisp and pleasant.

He liked this place but . . . it took him a moment to recognize what was different about this nameless saloon in the middle of nowhere.

46

There were no women.

No whores. No female dealers with low-cut blouses to distract the bettors. No dancers or singers or entertainers of any sort. Not even a piano player, male or female.

It was a place for men only. Men who wanted to drink and talk and gamble quietly and without raising a ruckus.

This was definitely not what he might have expected.

Pete came down the length of his well behind the bar. He stopped in front of Longarm and leaned forward to nod over Longarm's shoulder and say, "Mr. Jiggs would like to welcome you to Yesterday, Curtis."

"Who is? . . ."

"Mr. Jiggs is that gentleman at the table in the front corner over there. He's the, uh, larger gentleman facing this way."

Larger was one way of putting it. Hog fat would have been more accurate. Longarm suspected the man would not fit into a beer barrel if you stripped him naked and greased him to ease the way.

Jiggs saw Longarm glance in his direction. He solemnly nodded, then looked back at the cards he was holding.

Obviously, Longarm thought, this would be an audience with the king.

He tossed back the rest of his rye, picked up his beer mug, and ambled across the room to Mr. Jiggs's table.

Chapter 13

If a bullfrog could speak, it would sound like Mr. Jiggs. Deep. Slow. Gravelly. "Welcome to Yesterday, Mr. London. I am Mr. Jiggs." His chins quivered and flowed when he spoke, but his lips barely moved. "Sit down. Would you like anything? A refill perhaps? Something to eat?"

"I'm fine, thanks. I just finished supper."

"At the café. Of course."

"I see you've been told my name, Mr. Jiggs. What's yours, if you don't mind me askin'? Your first name, I mean."

"You can just call me Mr. Jiggs. Everyone does."

"Yes, sir. I, uh, I was advised to see you if I wanted t' do any business here."

"A mere formality," Mr. Jiggs said with a smile. The smile, Longarm noticed, did not reach his eyes. Those remained cold and calculating. There were no laugh wrinkles around them.

But then, Longarm thought, perhaps there was too much fat stuffed beneath his skin to allow for the formation of wrinkles.

The man had good skin. Smooth and rosy like a baby's butt.

"I always like to greet newcomers," Mr. Jiggs said. "I would not want anyone to get off on the wrong foot, so let me make this clear. A man is allowed to conduct business in Yesterday to his heart's content. Hopefully, to his betterment as well. Profit, after all, is what makes the world go around.

"You should understand," he went on, "that this is my town. I set the rules. Residents obey them or they are . . . invited to leave." The false smile flashed again. Longarm wondered just what sort of "invitation" was issued when someone was told to leave.

"Yesterday gives a man great profit potential because, you see, one does not have to be in competition here. You may already have noticed that Yesterday has one café. One saloon only. One hotel. One general store. One feed store. One livery. One whorehouse. I license these businesses, Mr. London. I assure business owners they will have a monopoly. You understand what a monopoly is, I would assume?"

"Yes, sir, I do."

"Yes, of course. I did not mean to slight you. We do sometimes receive business—shall we say—'applicants' who do not comprehend the advantages of a monopoly." The smile appeared again and as quickly retreated.

Mr. Jiggs said, "I understand you are a broker, Mr. London. You deal in wholesale commodities? Arrange freight transport? Things like that?"

"Exactly," Longarm said. Who the hell had he told he was a broker? It took him a moment to recall his idle comment to that effect. He had mentioned it to one of the men sitting at his table in the café. Somehow that information had already reached Mr. Jiggs. Longarm was impressed.

"As it happens," Mr. Jiggs said, "our resident businessmen have been arranging their buying piecemeal, dealing with one company or another as far away as Missouri or California. A broker might well be of use to them." The smile came. Went. "If I approve of the terms of your business dealings, Mr. London, I will offer you a license. Your initial license will be for three months. After that, your performance will be reviewed. Hopefully, I will approve of what you are doing here and you will be given a renewal on a more permanent basis."

"And the cost of this license?" Longarm asked.

"The same as every other business pays, Mr. London. One hundred dollars per month."

"That seems . . . quite a lot," Longarm said.

"It is, however, a monopoly. And every business in town will be obligated to make their purchases through you." This time the smile remained.

Longarm whistled. "A monopoly *and* every firm in town deals with me? If I may say so, Mr. Jiggs, a hundred dollars seems a modest amount on those terms."

"Then we are agreed?"

"Would you mind if I think about this for a day or two? One of the things I was taught at an early age is to never plunge into anything, no matter how good it sounds."

"I don't mind at all," Mr. Jiggs said. "Take your time. Take as much as, oh, four days to think it over. At the end of that time we will either shake hands on a deal profitable to each of us, or you will be asked to leave Yesterday."

"Four days. Starting"—Longarm pulled the Ingersoll from his vest pocket and glanced at the time—"starting now?"

"Starting now," Mr. Jiggs agreed.

Longarm shoved back from the table and stood. Off to one side, there were a pair of men hunched over fans of cards. They appeared to be playing gin rummy, but their attention was on Mr. Jiggs and on this visitor to the community.

Both of them were heeled, Longarm saw. He got the impression that either of them could get his pistol out on the double-quick if need be.

"Thank you for your time, Mr. Jiggs, and for the drink." He smiled, Longarm's smile not touching his eyes any more than Mr. Jiggs's had. "We'll talk again later."

Mr. Jiggs had already dismissed Curtis London from mind and was concentrating on the cards in his hand.

Chapter 14

Two hours of poker had Longarm thirty-some dollars ahead. He was not quite sure if he'd legitimately won that much, or if he was winning on Mr. Jiggs's orders to soften him up so he would be inclined to favor the deal Mr. Jiggs offered.

If the games were rigged, though, the cheating was done mighty damn well. Longarm could generally spot card-sharps and wheels that did not run true. Here, he could see nothing wrong.

Which did not, of course, mean that nothing *was* wrong, only that he could not *see* anything out of line.

After a while, he accepted that and cashed out. He tipped the dealer a dollar, finished his last whiskey, and made his way back to the hotel.

Nothing in his room was out of place. Everything looked exactly as it should. Yet he had the impression that someone had gone through his bag while he was out of the room. It was almost like there was a scent in the room that . . . He stopped. Inhaled slowly and deeply.

Someone had indeed been in the room. He was sure of it, someone who smelled of something sweet. Not bay rum, but something on that order. It was nothing—no one—he had smelled before. But if he found that scent again, he would recognize it.

Longarm undressed quickly and crawled into the crude bed gratefully. It had been a long day and a worrisome one, his biggest worry at the moment being how best he should approach the problem at hand. Passing himself off as a commodities broker had advantages, but it also meant he had to be cautious about what he asked and how he asked it.

Perhaps the best course would be to sleep on it and let his subconscious take over.

He was asleep practically before his head hit the pillow.

Breakfast was hotcakes, ham, and redeye gravy. It just didn't get much better than that. He filled up on it, then lingered for a spell over coffee until the Mexican owner began to openly scowl. There were others who wanted that seat at the table, and usually Longarm would have cleared out in a hurry. This time, he had a reason to delay. When he came into the café, the businesses along the main street were all still closed.

By the time he was done cooling his heels—without being evicted from the café—the door of the general store, the business the town had grown around, was open. Most of the buildings in town were constructed of sawed lumber. The general store was in a log structure. Longarm stepped up onto the board sidewalk in front and went inside.

The man behind the counter was on the gray-haired side of middle age. What little hair he had left, that is, was gray. He only had a fringe remaining. There was no way to tell what color his hair once had been.

"Can I help you, Mr. London?"

"How would you . . ." Longarm shook his head and

smiled. "Never mind. I understand. But may I have the pleasure of knowing who I'm speaking with here?"

The proprietor stuck his hand out to shake. "Sam Pendergast," he said. "Pleasure, sir. Now what is it I can do for you, Mr. London?"

"If you already know my name, then I suppose you know why I'm here."

Pendergast nodded. "Indeed I do. It makes sense. One broker for the needs of all. Able to consolidate freight charges. Yes, I'd say it makes sense. But you understand, of course, that none of us can talk business with you unless you agree to participate in our little, um, enterprise."

"I realize that, of course," Longarm said. Not that he had realized any such thing, but then, what the hell did he know about business or businessmen? He pursed his lips in thought for a moment, then smiled. "Enterprise. Is that what you call it?"

The storekeeper shrugged. "It's as good a term as any, I suppose. Enterprise. Communal endeavor. The point is that it works."

"One for all and all for one, is that right?"

"So it is, Mr. London, so it is. But since we can't conduct any business here, what can I do for you?"

"Two things," Longarm said. "First, I may be wanting to submit orders and give instructions over the telegraph. Does your store have the wire for Yesterday?"

"Goodness, no. The closest telegraph is in Buffalo. I don't exactly know why they've never strung a wire in here, but we're still waiting."

That surprised Longarm. *Some*one had sent the wire that brought him here. It had not been signed, but he had hoped to find the Good Samaritan who sent it.

On the other hand, looking at it from the optimistic

point of view, there not being a telegraph in Yesterday relieved him of the responsibility to let Billy Vail and Henry know where he was and when he might be back.

"There was something else?" Pendergast asked.

"Hmm?"

"Two questions, you said."

"Oh. Right. Thanks for reminding me." Longarm patted his chest pocket. "I was wonderin' if you carry cheroots. I might be running low, dependin' on how long I stay here. I can make do with regular cigars an' I've been known to stoop as low as smoking crooks when I have to, but those little dark tobacco New Orleans cheroots are my preference when I can get 'em."

Pendergast smiled. "You are in luck, Mr. London. I have some of the finest cheroots you will ever find. Mr. Jiggs smokes them, you see, and Mr. Jiggs enjoys nothing but the best."

"In that case, sir, I'll take a dollar's worth." Longarm pulled out one of the silver dollars he'd won at poker the night before. He laid it on the counter. "Come to think of it, take out five cents of that for matches."

Longarm lighted one of his fresh-bought cheroots as soon as he exited the store. He stopped under the roof overhang to puff on his smoke—it was every bit as good as Pendergast said it would be—and ponder the fact that there was no telegraph in Yesterday.

After a few moments, he stepped down from the sidewalk and went to see if Yesterday had a barbershop. Just one, of course. The town barber would not be wanting competition. Mr. Jiggs's rule.

Chapter 15

A telegraph will carry news from elsewhere, but a barber-shop had all the news about local events. Fistfight? Birth? Wedding plans? For that matter, someone's daughter getting knocked up by the boy next door? The town barber will be among the first to hear about it. He might or might not talk about it, but he will almost certainly hear about it.

The sign painted onto a window of this shop announced: HAROLD MOORE, BARBER. Longarm paused beside the window to take a few last puffs on his cheroot, then tossed it into the street. He went inside. There were two men ahead of him.

"Good morning, Mr. London," the barber said, looking up from the man in his chair.

"Good morning. You'd be Mr. Moore?"

"I am, sir. What can I do for you?"

"A trim an' a shave, I think," Longarm said.

"Yes, sir. Have a seat there. I won't be long."

There were magazines and several newspapers scattered on the chairs. Longarm picked up a newspaper—it was the current week's edition of the *Buffalo Plain Speaker*—and nodded a greeting to the other patrons. They were engrossed in their reading, but took a moment to nod in return. Longarm sat as close to the barber chair as he could get. So he could hear everything that was said.

An hour or more later, he had not learned anything of interest, although he did know now what the local "experts" thought the weather would be during this growing season and what the territorial legislature was up to lately. It was all very exciting stuff. Longarm yawned and eased into the chair as soon as the barber called his name.

"A trim and a shave, you said?"

"Yes, sir."

Moore began snipping away at Longarm's hair.

"Say, maybe you could tell me something," Longarm said.

"If I know, certainly."

"I'm wonderin' just how safe this town is. I mean, sometimes I carry large amounts o' money. Is there a sheriff or a deputy or something?"

"We had a town marshal for a while," Moore said, "but . . ." He hesitated for a moment. "I hate to tell you this, but the truth is, our marshal was murdered."

"That don't sound good."

"Don't misunderstand. Yesterday is normally a very peaceful place, but Franklin—that was his name, James Franklin—he was murdered one night. No one knows who did it or why."

"Belligerent sort o' fellow, this James Franklin?" Longarm asked. Jim Franklin had been calm and patient. Very deliberate in his investigations and careful with his conclusions. Lord knows he had been calm and patient with a young fellow named Custis Long.

"Oh, no. Just the opposite," Moore said. "He was a retired fella. I forget what he done before he came here. Where he did it, I mean. I think he was an officer of the law for most of his life. Though he did mention farming in Indiana when he was a boy. I think his people are still on the land back there."

That was right. Longarm reminded himself to send a sympathy card to Jim's sister. What the hell was her name now? She'd married and had a couple kids. Jim's nephews, those would be. Longarm wanted to be able to tell them all that Jim Franklin's murderer had been brought to justice.

"When did this happen?" Longarm asked. He already knew the answer. It happened when he was close by in Leon County after delivering those prisoners.

It happened when he was wallowing in a hotel bed instead of riding over here to see Jim.

It happened because he was a lazy bastard who thought of himself first ahead of his friends.

It happened because Custis Long had not been here and ready to help a friend who was in need.

It happened.

But if Longarm had been here . . .

"Mr. London? Mr. London. Are you all right, Mr. London?"

"I . . . yeah. I'm fine, thanks." Longarm brought himself back from the churning memories and regrets that threatened to overwhelm him. "What is it, Mr. Moore?"

"I need for you to sit a little higher in the chair so I can shave you properly."

"Sure. Sorry."

The barber began briskly whipping up a lather in his soap mug.

Chapter 16

Somehow, it made Jim's murder more real now that he'd heard about it from strangers. From strangers Jim had protected with his life.

Well, Longarm intended to find the murderer or give his own life trying. Jim's killer would *not* walk away from this without paying.

Longarm walked away from the barbershop smelling of bay rum and scented talcum powder. His outlook was venomous. If he could confront the son of a bitch who murdered Jim Franklin . . .

That was the thing. Maybe he already had. He just did not know.

He headed for the livery. The proprietor was not there, so Longarm led the little mare out and fumbled with the unfamiliar harness, then hitched her into the curved poles of the driving rig.

He felt like a right proper dude sitting up there on the buggy seat with little to do but watch the world go by.

Inactivity can be bad for a man, though. It gave him too much time to think. To think about Jim Franklin and the fine man he had been. Dead now and buried.

Longarm was still thinking about Jim when he rolled into Buffalo ten hours later.

"Take care of your rig, mister?"

"Yes, thanks. Say, where can I find the telegraph office?"

"Right down the street. Next to the post office. But it's closed for the night now. I seen old Timothy heading home to his supper a little while ago."

Longarm checked his watch and glanced at the sky. It would be dark soon and while the road was in good shape and the ruts distinct, he did not think it would be sensible to drive back to Yesterday in the black of the night. That would be pushing the little mare too hard. Risking the wheels of the buggy, too. "Where can I find a room?"

"You might try the hotel," the fellow said, his expression so innocent that Longarm knew his leg was being pulled. But not unkindly. The man was just having a little fun.

"And that would be?"

The man grinned and chuckled a little, then gave directions.

Longarm hadn't thought to bring his carpetbag along. He hadn't expected to be overnight actually, but Buffalo—one of the prettiest little towns anywhere—was farther away than he'd realized. He decided to go arrange for a room before he disturbed the telegraph operator's evening.

He thanked the liveryman and paid him for one night, then walked over to the hotel.

"Yes, sir. We have a room vacant. Got a mighty fine restaurant, too. My missus does the cooking and I can tell you true, she knows how to make plain food sing and shout." The hotel proprietor, a white-haired man in sleeve garters, patted his ample belly by way of demonstration.

Food. Longarm's stomach rumbled in anticipation at the

thought. He had not gotten around to eating anything since breakfast, and it was around sundown now. "Where is?—"

"Right in through that door, Mr. . ." The hotel keeper spun the guest register around to face him and looked down at Longarm's signature. "Mr. London."

"Thanks."

Longarm followed his host's pointing finger—and his own nose—through the door indicated to a small dining area. It only had three tables. But then the hotel was small. It looked like it was originally built as a private residence and only later was turned into a hotel.

Of the three tables, only one was occupied, that by a woman who was engrossed in reading something at the side of her plate. Her bonnet obscured her features, but her slender figure and small size gave the impression that she was young.

And traveling alone?

He had to wonder if she was pretty.

Very deliberately, Longarm chose a seat immediately in front of her so that when she looked up from her book he would find out if she was attractive.

She heard the scrape of his chair or otherwise sensed his presence.

She looked up.

And Longarm inwardly groaned.

He was registered here under the name Curtis London. This was the same young woman he had traveled with on the stage up from Cheyenne. Did she know him as a deputy United States marshal named Long? He could not remember.

Damn!

When she saw him, she smiled. Said, "Hello, how are you? Do you know anyone in Buffalo? I don't. Are you dining alone? How sad. Here. Come sit with me while you have your dinner." She gestured toward the chair opposite hers.

His luck was not running worth a shit.

Longarm could think of no polite way to refuse. And she really wasn't bad-looking. He got up, moved to her table, and sat down again. He smiled at the young woman and nodded. "Ma'am."

If he could only remember if she might have heard his name . . .

Chapter 17

"It is such a lovely evening," she said when Longarm's meal was finished and the coffee cups had been cleared away.

"Yes. Very." Very ordinary was the truth of it, but if the girl wanted to think it was "lovely," well, fine. Who was he to argue the point?

"I would enjoy having a walk, but I don't think it would be seemly for a lady to walk alone in a strange town. One just never knows."

Buffalo was probably as safe a place as Longarm had ever been in. But then . . . who was he to argue the point?

Besides, it was not nervousness about being alone in a strange town that she meant. He understood that. "May I escort you?" he offered.

Her smile was her answer.

It was, in fact, a pretty nice evening. The air was crisp and clean. The water in the nearby creek chuckled and danced. The stars looked like someone had turned up the wicks and made them all brighter than usual.

Longarm paused on the porch to light a cheroot, then

offered his arm and led the girl down to the footbridge across the creek.

"Can we stop here for a moment?" she asked when they reached the middle of the little bridge.

They turned and leaned on the rail, faces lifted to a fresh breeze coming downstream. "It is lovely," she said.

"Yes, it is." He was not speaking about the evening, though.

There was no moon yet, but there was enough starlight to clearly show her features, soft and rounded.

"Would you think it bold of me to ask you something?" she said.

"Ask anything you like," Longarm said.

"Are you married?"

That was *not* the question he expected. "Uh . . . no. Why d'you ask?"

She smiled quite sweetly. "Because I would like to fuck you."

It was a good thing he had the bridge rail to hang on to or he might have toppled into the water. As it was, he tossed what remained of his cheroot into the creek and grinned at her. "Your room or mine?"

The young woman shocked him for the second time by replying, "Neither." She giggled, sounding like a schoolgirl let out for recess.

What she did next was most definitely not the action of a schoolgirl, though. She leaned over the bridge rail, arms folded and head out over the water. That put her butt up in the air. She looked back at Longarm and said, "I'm not wearing any pantaloons. Lift my skirt and let me feel what you have."

"Here? Out in public?"

"That's right. Right here. Right now. Let me have it."

"What if somebody comes along?"

"We can worry about that if it happens. If it doesn't . . ." She shrugged. "Why worry?"

Longarm hesitated. The girl reached over to his crotch and fondled him. His pecker immediately rose to the occasion, and she giggled with delight. "Beautiful," she said, and began undoing the buttons of his fly.

"Stand behind me now. Close. That's good." She gave him an encouraging squeeze, and used her hold on his cock to pull him into place where she wanted him. "Now lift my skirt and drape it between us. Yes, perfect." She laughed. "I think now you should be able to manage the next step on your own."

He could.

With her hand still guiding him, he found the bushy entrance he sought. He pushed, and his pole slid readily into the already wet depths. She surrounded him with her flesh.

The girl pushed back hard against him, clenching her teeth and moaning as he filled her, pulled back slightly, then rammed hard forward, almost lifting her off her toes. She grunted, then wriggled her hips.

"Yesssss," she hissed. "Hard. Harder. Hurt me with it if you can."

He couldn't. But he tried. He slammed into her as hard as he was able, driving her up against the bridge rail. Again. Again.

She cried out, and he was reminded for a moment that they were in a public place in the early evening and anyone could be about.

The feeling inside her was too good to stop, though. Even had someone walked by, he was not sure he could stop. As it was, a stray dog walked up to them and sat hoping for a handout, but no humans accompanied the animal, and Longarm did not break the rhythm of his stroking to pay attention to the dog.

The pressure built and built to a fantastic level—aided all the more by the danger of discovery perhaps—until he could contain it no longer.

His release squirted hot and sticky into her, and she cried out in response to her own sudden climax.

Both of them were left weak and with trembling legs when he finally withdrew. She smoothed the hem of her dress down and tucked him back inside his britches, not seeming to mind in the slightest that she got her hands wet and gooey in the process.

When she was done and his trousers were again presentable in public, she gave him an impish smile . . . and licked his fluids from her fingers. Slowly. Savoring the scents and flavors that came off him.

Then, as if nothing at all had happened, she said, "I believe I've walked enough this evening. Would you escort me back to the hotel, please? I believe I would like to retire now."

Longarm touched the brim of his Stetson and half-bowed. "Yes, ma'am. Happy to."

No one seeing the two of them return to the hotel could have guessed. He hoped.

Chapter 18

"Good morning." Her smile was sweet and innocent. She looked very much the virgin when she came down for breakfast. "Please join me."

"I've already had my breakfast," he said. "I was just on my way out t' take care of some business."

"Can it wait a few minutes?" she asked, laying the tips of her fingers lightly on the back of his wrist. Her eyes were large and imploring. Her smile became even sweeter if that were possible. How could he say no?

"I could stand another cup o' coffee."

"Thank you." The girl did not wait for him. She led the way into the otherwise empty dining room and stood aside, confident he would hold a chair for her. He did.

Anyone watching would think they were barely acquainted, he was sure.

"A bowl of oatmeal, please. And tea with lemon. Nothing else," she told the lady who came to wait on them.

"Coffee refill for you, sir?"

"Yes, thanks," Longarm said.

When the waitress disappeared into the kitchen, the girl leaned forward. In a whisper, she said, "I asked who you are. Imagine my surprise to discover you registered as a business traveler named London. Imagine that . . . Marshal Long."

"Look, I, uh . . ."

"Oh, there is no need for you to worry . . . *Mr*. London. I'll not give you away."

Longarm frowned and paused for only a moment, then said, "You want somethin'."

The smile flashed again, every bit as bright. "But of course I do, dear man. A favor for a favor. It's all very simple."

"And what you're askin' is? . . ." He let the question hang in the air between them.

The waitress came back with coffee for Longarm and tea for the lady. The girl waited until she was gone before replying. "All I ask from you is . . . discretion."

Longarm raised his eyebrows but he said nothing.

The girl went on. "When you left the coach a few days ago, at that stage station . . ."

"I remember," he said.

"You asked the station keeper about transportation to Yesterday."

Longarm nodded. "That's right."

"That will be where you came from. May I assume you will be returning there? I would think so. Otherwise, why keep the false name?"

"I'll be goin' back," Longarm conceded.

"I want to ride with you."

"What the? . . ."

"Yesterday is my destination. I only stopped here to rest for a few days before going on." She frowned. "It is terribly wearing, maintaining a false front."

"I don't know what you mean about that."

She batted her eyelashes, deliberately overdoing it, and applied a very thick Southern accent. "Why, suh, can't you see that Ah am a young and innocent virgin?"

Longarm's sudden laugh came out like a bark. So much so that the waitress peered around the doorjamb to see what was wrong. "I just swallowed wrong," Longarm said by way of apology, blaming his as yet untasted cup of coffee for the noise. He leaned close to the girl and whispered, "If you say so, honey."

"That is another thing," she returned, in her own voice again. "While we have met, if barely, you do know that my name is Glenda Bateman. You know me well enough to speak to me as Miss Glenda. Nothing more familiar, please."

That was interesting. He hadn't had a fucking clue what her name was until now. And from the way she said it, he suspected that Glenda Bateman was not the same name he might have overheard on the ride up here on the stagecoach. "Uh-huh. A virgin, you say."

She giggled. "Oh, yes. And he will believe it, too. I have a little vial of sheep's blood and some crystals of alum with me."

"The sheep's blood I understand, but what's the alum for?"

She giggled again. He really wished she would stop that. He did not want to hear it all the way back to Yesterday. "It tightens things up. It will make me smaller. Down there, I mean. Believe me, when he has me, he will be convinced he's having a virgin."

"An' who is this lucky 'he' that you're talkin' about?"

She shrugged. "I'm really not sure. An older gentleman, I presume." Giggle. "The one thing I am sure of is that his check was good. It has already been deposited into my account back home." She did not care to offer exactly where that might be, and Longarm did not care to ask. "His name is Benito Jiggs." Giggle. "Doesn't he just sound like a little ol' darlin'?"

Surprise, Longarm thought. But he said nothing about the "little ol' darlin'." Like the girl said, Mr. Jiggs's money was already in her bank. It seemed that Mr. Benito Jiggs had bought himself a virgin. Reckon the joke was on him.

"All right, it's a deal," Longarm said. "I'll keep shut about what I know 'bout you an' you do the same for me."

He offered his hand, and they shook on their agreement.

Miss Glenda's oatmeal arrived, and Longarm shoved his chair back from the table, standing and reaching for his hat. "If you'll excuse me, Miss Glenda, I'd best be about the business that brought me here."

"You will let me know when you are ready to leave."

"Of course." He bowed, turned, and strode out of there.

A virgin. Again. Be damned!

Chapter 19

Buffalo's telegraph office was easy enough to find. He simply crossed the creek to reach the main business street, then looked for wires strung above the ground. He found one. It led to one of the two stagecoach operators doing business in the community, this one owned by the Overland Express Company. It was next door to the post office, just like the fellow at the livery had said.

The clerk inside was not the old-timer Longarm had been given to expect. Instead, this was a youngster probably not yet out of his teen years. He was not even old enough to shave yet.

"Are you the stationmaster?" Longarm asked once inside the office.

The boy laughed. "No, sir. Mr. Timothy is over to the café having coffee with some of his friends. But I can sell you a ticket if that's what you need or answer most questions you might have."

"I do have a question," Longarm said. "About a week, week an' a half ago, someone sent a message from here addressed to Denver an' telling about the town marshal down in Yesterday bein' murdered. D'you recall a wire like that going out?"

"I'm sorry, sir, but telegraph messages are private. They're regarded the same as mail. I can't tell you what was sent from here or what wasn't. Sorry."

Longarm wasted a few moments getting a cheroot out and lighting it while he considered whether he should trust this wet-behind-the-ears kid with knowledge that could be disastrous to his investigation if it got back to Yesterday. Down there he was Curtis London, commodities broker. He would have preferred to remain that here, too.

Eventually, he reached the inevitable conclusion that he simply had no choice.

Besides, Glenda Bateman already knew who he was. Why shouldn't this youngster join the parade? He reached inside his coat and brought out his wallet, flipping it open to display his badge.

"I'm a deputy United States marshal, son. An' I need that information."

The boy's eyes grew wide. He leaned forward across the counter and peered closely at Longarm's badge. "I never saw one of those before. How do I know it's real?"

"Because it has the power to put you behind bars for ten days for obstruction of justice if you refuse to cooperate with me here." That was pure bullshit, but he was assuming the youngster would not know that.

The kid backed away from the counter and thought for a moment, then said, "What was it you wanted to know, sir?"

"Before we get into that, you know how important it is t' keep your mouth shut about the message traffic that flows through here. Well, it's even more important that you don't tell anybody about who I really am or what I ask you. I'm travelin' incognito here, pretendin' to be somebody else,

74

and it wouldn't please me none to learn you been talking out o' school."

"I know how to stay shut, Marshal."

"Good. Now tell me who it was as sent that message to me down in Denver."

"It was you who got that?"

Longarm nodded. "My real name is Custis Long. That's the way the message was addressed."

"I remember. We get a fair amount of traffic through here, but not so much going to U.S. marshals that I could forget one. You want to know about the death notice for Marshal Franklin. He wasn't, uh, one of you guys, was he?"

"A federal deputy? No. Jim Franklin was just what he seemed t' be, an old lawman who didn't have no pension to retire on so he was still working in his old age."

"I see. Well . . . you already know what was in that message if, like you claim, you're the one it went to."

"I know exactly what was in it, son. What I need from you is t' know who sent it."

"Oh, I don't, um, know his name or anything."

"It was a man, though."

"Yes, sir."

"Young? Old? What'd he look like?"

"He was an older gentleman. About this tall." The boy indicated with his hand. "He was bald, I remember that much about him. I don't think I ever saw him before, though."

"He didn't give a name?"

The young telegrapher shook his head. "No, sir, he did not."

Older. Bald. Name unknown. It was not much to go on.

On the other hand, it was more than Longarm had known when he walked in here. "Thanks." He continued to stand at the counter, indecisive.

"Is there something else, Marshal?"

"Yeah, I, uh, reckon I'd best send a wire o' my own. Let the office know where I am. Take this down, please. Address it to U.S. Marshal William Vail, Federal Building, Denver, Colorado. I want the text t' read . . ."

Five minutes later, he walked out of the express company office and headed for the livery stable where he had left his hired buggy.

If pressed on the subject, he might have had to admit that the thought at least crossed his mind to leave Glenda Bateman sitting right where she was in a Buffalo hotel. To do so would very likely be doing her a favor. After all, he had seen Mr. Jiggs. Glenda had not.

The thought of that mountain of fatty flesh naked and amorous . . . poor Glenda.

Come to think of it, how the hell did somebody that big manage to get himself laid? Oh, finding a woman was the easy part. Money took care of that. But just exactly how did he . . . Keep on visualizing shit like that, Longarm figured, and soon Glenda wouldn't be the only one who was breaking out in giggles.

Lordy, he was just glad he would not have to watch. Nor to hear the girl tell about it afterward.

He was chuckling when he reached the livery stable.

Chapter 20

"Why are we stopping here?" Glenda asked when Longarm pulled the mare to a halt outside one of Buffalo's mercantiles.

"Grub," he told her. "Slow as it is t' travel in a wheeled rig, we'll be overnight. Likely reach Yesterday mid-morning tomorrow."

"We could push straight through if we had to, couldn't we?"

Longarm shrugged. "This ain't an emergency."

The girl sniffed. "Humph. You just want to get into my bloomers again."

"As I recall, you don't wear 'em," Longarm said. "But I would admit that the thought crossed my mind."

She giggled. Lordy, was he going to have to put up with that all the way to Yesterday? Maybe he should push the mare through anyway. On the other hand . . .

"How's your trail camp cooking, little lady?"

"Cooking? Good heavens, if I knew how to cook I wouldn't be selling myself to strangers." Giggle. "Well, maybe I would at that. But I would at least be able to consider alternatives. Wouldn't I?"

"How'd you get hooked up with Mr. Jiggs anyhow, Miss Glenda?"

"I was working in a whorehouse in New Orleans. A lawyer representing Mr. Jiggs posted notices in the newspaper there seeking an adventurous virgin. He wanted someone young and attractive. Which I try to be. And, um, certain events had recently taken place that made it a very good idea for me to leave the house and find opportunity elsewhere." She smiled. "Forgive me if I fail to elaborate on that."

"No offense taken, Miss Glenda."

"There were several of us interviewed for the position. The lawyer—he is a very nice man, I must say, and very grateful for any small favors a girl might perform—selected me. He is the one who released the payment."

"Has the check already cleared the bank?"

"Oh, yes. I insisted on that. The nice lawyer was agreeable. He helped me expi . . . expa . . ."

"Expedite?" Longarm suggested.

Glenda clapped her hands. "Expedite. Yes. Thank you. He helped me to get the check cleared and my funds on deposit."

"How long is your contract, if you don't mind me askin'? How long 've you been paid for?"

"Oh, for a year. I am paid up for the next whole year."

Longarm shook his head, marveling at the audacity of the girl. "You got all your virgin-makin' stuff with you?"

"Right in my bag ready for use," she assured him.

"Is there anything you need?"

"I can't think of anything."

"Getting back t' the original subject, what d'you want in the way of trail grub?"

"I . . . wouldn't know exactly what trail grub might be," Glenda admitted.

"Jerky mostly," Longarm said. "Or old biscuits crumbled into coffee and et like a soup. That sort o' thing."

Glenda made a sour face. "Nothing civilized?"

Longarm shook his head. "Not unless you cook it."

The grimace flashed again. "Could we pack a picnic? Sort of?"

"We'll do the best we can with whatever they're sellin' inside here," Longarm said, wrapping the driving lines around the whip socket and climbing down from the buggy.

He went around to the passenger side of the little rig and helped Glenda step down. Then the two of them went inside to see what they could find in the way of food to sustain them overnight.

Chapter 21

"How 'bout this?" Longarm asked. If there was a hint of impatience in his voice, well, this was the third place he had suggested they stop for the night.

The first had been too steep. The second too rocky. This one, he hoped, would be just right. It had good grass for the mare, a stand of trees, even a small brook running down out of the Big Horns. If they did not stop here, they might as well travel on into the night until they reached Yesterday.

Glenda pursed her lips and furrowed her brow in deep consideration. Then she nodded. "This will do," she announced.

Longarm managed to contain an impulse to shout "Hosanna." All he said was, "Stay there. I'll help you down."

He did, then unhitched the mare and hobbled her before turning her loose to graze and to drink. He tossed the harness into the buggy and fetched the sack of eatables they had purchased back in Buffalo.

He did not know about Glenda Bateman, but he himself was damned well hungry. Lunch had been an apple and a wedge of rat cheese. Those were good, but they were not food to sustain a man.

"Hungry?" he asked.

The girl surprised him. "I could eat that horse if you would just shoot him for me."

"First off, he's a girl horse. Second, if I shoot her an' cook her for supper, you'll have t' walk the rest o' the way."

"Oh, I was just teasing. But I would like to have a good meal tonight. Once we reach Yesterday, I have to be the proper little virgin with my best Southern manners on display. I must eat like a bird and speak ever so softly."

"It must be hard t' have to playact all the time with never a break so's you can be yourself. You know. Scratch an' fart an' all those things."

"Gracious, Mr. London, a lady *never* does anything so vulgar as that."

"Like I say. Must be hard."

Now that they found their spot to camp overnight, there was no need to rush. Longarm put a stew together—apparently Glenda honestly did not know anything about cooking—with potatoes, carrots, and chunks of pork brought from Buffalo, all boiled together in a pot. When the food was thoroughly cooked, he piled the meat and vegetables on a square of oilcloth and added a handful of flour to the water to make a gravy, then put everything back into the pot and stirred it around.

"There. As fine a sonuvabitch stew as ever you'll throw a lip over."

"Are you being deliberately crude, Mr. London?"

"Perhaps. A little. But I think you'll forgive me once you have a taste o' my stew. Now grab you one o' those plates an' a spoon. An', Miss Glenda . . ."

"Yes, Mr. London?"

"I done the cooking, so after supper you can clean up."

"Where?"

Silently, he pointed to the little creek that trickled past.

Glenda sighed. But she ate enough for three men and a boy, Longarm noticed, so she must not have been too put out by his demand.

And after supper, she did indeed wash everything, scrubbing the plates and pot and utensils with the coarse sand she collected from the icy cold run of water.

"All done?" he asked. The sun had long since disappeared and there was a chill in the air. The only light showing was their fire, which he was allowing to burn low now.

Glenda nodded.

"You say you got your virgin kit in that bag there?"

"Yes, of course."

"Well, forget the blood. We don't need none o' that. But . . . it's been an awful long time since I had a virgin. Would you might be usin' that . . . what'd you say that stuff is?"

She laughed. "Alum. It is called alum, Mr. London, and I shall be glad to be a virgin for you."

Damned if she wasn't, too. By the time she was ready for him, she was so tight they had to lubricate his pole before he could force it into her. Any sort of oil or grease would work, she said, then added, "But plain old saliva is as good as anything."

Saying that, and giggling, she took him into her mouth.

The girl was right. A simple application of spit worked just fine to let him slide inside her body. And she really was as tight as a virgin.

If a man was expecting virginity, he would find it.

Longarm laughed, then gave the girl his weight and began pumping inside that slender body.

Yes, sir, it had been a genuinely long time since Custis Long had a virgin under him. He almost forgot how good it was. Until now. Glenda reminded him.

Chapter 22

"D'you want t' go to the hotel first so's you can freshen up?" Longarm asked as the buggy rolled into Yesterday.

Glenda shook her head. "No. Benny . . . that is what I call him, Benny, short for Benito . . . Benny said he would have accommodations for me above his business palace. That is what he called it. A 'business palace.' Which sounded odd, but what does an innocent virgin know about business?" She giggled.

The girl was a good fuck, with or without that virgin-making stuff, but he *did* wish she would put a cork in all the giggling.

Longarm guided the mare in the direction of Mr. Jiggs's saloon and idly asked, "Did Benny send you a picture of himself? A photograph or any sort o' representation?"

She shook her head again. "No. Why do you ask?"

"Just curious. Whoa, horse." Longarm's hands tightened on the driving lines, and the little mare obediently came to a halt beside the boardwalk in front of the saloon. "Wait there."

Longarm jumped down from the buggy, clipped a hitch weight to the mare's bit, then handed Glenda down onto the boards. Once she was safely on her feet, he fetched her bags from the back of the rig and said, "I can carry these inside for you if you like, Miss Glenda."

She smiled—she had dimples when she did that—and said, "You are very kind, Mr. London. Yes, thank you."

The plain truth was that Longarm would have found some excuse to go inside anyway. He really wanted to see Glenda Bateman's reaction when she got her first look at Mr. Benito Jiggs.

"After you, miss," he said, picking up her bags and trailing along behind the girl.

Mr. Jiggs was at his usual place, sitting behind his favorite table with a few sycophants surrounding him and his cold-eyed bodyguards positioned close by.

When it became clear just which one of the cardplayers was Mr. Jiggs, Longarm heard a sudden intake of breath from Glenda. Nothing more. He guessed her training in a New Orleans whorehouse must have helped.

But, Lordy, Mr. Jiggs would make four of her. Six maybe. Yet the girl did not appear to turn a hair. In fact, she put her sweetest and most dimpled smile on her face. Longarm rather admired her for that.

"You all right, girl?"

She nodded. "Yes. Thank you." She looked and sounded a mite brittle, but the dimples never disappeared. Damn girl was better than he'd been giving her credit for.

"Want me t' make the introductions?"

"That would be nice, thank you."

He set her bags down by the stairs leading to a second floor, where he assumed they would be wanted later, then offered his arm to her. Glenda gave it a little squeeze and nodded a go-ahead to him.

"Mr. Jiggs, may I have the honor to introduce to you

Miss Glenda Bateman, late of New Orleans. Miss Bateman, the gentleman is Mr. Jiggs."

Mr. Jiggs struggled to his feet. It was not an easy task for a man of his bulk. Seeing him on his own hind legs like that, Longarm judged his weight to be somewhere around six hundred pounds . . . give or take a hundredweight.

Again, the image of Mr. Jiggs on top of Miss Bateman came unbidden into Longarm's mind. Hell, the man must be hung like a horse just to have enough pecker length to clear that belly and have enough left over to poke a girl.

It was all Longarm could do to keep from bursting out laughing.

"Sit down please, Miss Glenda."

Longarm dutifully held a chair for her. Once the girl was properly seated, Mr. Jiggs said, "Thank you for your help, Mr. London. Please have yourself some refreshment now. On the house." In other words, "Get the hell away from here."

Longarm bowed to the "lady"—never mind that she was no lady—and nodded his thanks to Mr. Jiggs.

He never saw the signal that Mr. Jiggs must have given to his bartender, but by the time Longarm reached the bar there was already a glass of excellent Maryland rye whiskey sitting on it and a freshly drawn beer chaser beside it. Mr. Jiggs, it seemed, ran a well-ordered ship.

Chapter 23

Longarm drove back to the livery, stripped the harness off the mare and put her into a stall, then wheeled the buggy around back. The gimpy hostler was nowhere in sight, so Longarm threw a fork of hay to the mare and walked down to the café.

"What are you serving for lunch?" he asked the Mexican proprietor.

The man grunted and scratched himself, then said, "Hot or cold?"

"What's the difference?"

"Ten cents."

"Hot," Longarm told him.

"Stew. It's fresh made."

Longarm nodded—the man made good stews, as he already knew—and forked over a quarter. In advance. The stew was every bit as good as he expected, although he was not entirely sure he wanted to know what the pale, slightly grainy meat in it was. Some things are best left unknown.

After he ate, he took a walk through the town, stopping in at each business he came to on the pretext of saying hello and getting acquainted. That seemed the sort of thing a businessman might do, he reasoned. What he was hoping to find, of course, was the bald man who sent that wire to him from Buffalo.

Unfortunately, a good many of the men in Yesterday were bald. Not a statistically high percentage, he supposed, but at least a dozen that he saw. And he could not always tell if a man had hair on top, not if the fellow happened to be wearing a hat.

"I seen your mare was back," the hostler said when Longarm returned to the livery.

"That's right."

"You owe me for her keep, mister. In advance, remember?"

"How could I forget that. I swear, it seems everybody in this town wants to be paid in advance. I hear it everywhere I go."

"You'll keep on hearing it, too. We got to mind our profits. By now I expect you know why."

"Yes, sir, I expect that I do." Longarm dug into his pocket and paid for another two days for the mare. He was running short on cash now, though, and would have been flat broke if it hadn't been for his winnings at the poker table a few nights ago. He hadn't really appreciated until now how easy it was to just show his badge and sign a payment voucher whenever he wanted something. This trip was coming out of his own pocket.

Not that he minded that. But, dammit, he hadn't thought to go to the bank for a wad of cash before he lit out from Denver.

Oh, well. He had until tomorrow around sundown to tell Mr. Jiggs if he was in or out as the town's commodities broker. He had enough to make it through until then.

"Something else I can do for you?" the hostler asked.

Longarm peered at the man. He had yet to see the fellow without his hat. And it was his experience that a good many old-time cowmen went bald. Something to do with the life, he supposed, his own theory being that wearing a good hat almost around the clock had something to do with it. Blocked the hair from getting air or something. At least that was what he guessed.

The gent gave no indication he was going to take the hat off, and it would have been a bit on the rude side of things for Longarm to step over to him and knock it off his head. "Nothing, thanks."

Longarm stepped outside and paused to light a cheroot— lighting up inside the stable with all the flammable straw and grain dust would have been worse than merely rude— then surveyed the length of Yesterday.

He had been inside every business in town without getting any closer to the man who sent that telegram. What he really had hoped was that the bald messenger would somehow give himself away.

That had not happened, but there was another card he could play.

He headed down the street to the old general store, the original building around which Yesterday had grown.

Chapter 24

"Who was Jim Franklin's executor?" Longarm asked.

"What do you mean?"

"Who is legally appointed to handle his estate? Surely somebody is."

"Now why would a stranger be wanting to know that?" merchant Leroy Bibbins asked. Bibbins was the fourth Yesterday storekeeper Longarm had spoken with on the subject. The conversation had gone pretty much the same in every other place.

"I just come back from Buffalo. The postmaster there asked me t' carry a envelope to whoever it is that's Marshal Franklin's executor."

"An envelope?"

Longarm nodded. "Yes, sir. A letter o' some sort addressed to a deputy U.S. marshal down in Denver."

"What does the letter say?"

Longarm shrugged. "Damned if I know. It ain't my letter so I ain't read it. I'm just carrying it down here for the man."

"Why would it come there to Buffalo anyway?"

Again the shrug. "Postmark says it was mailed from there. Rubber stamp on it says there's no such address as he put down. That's why it come back to Buffalo. I could figure out that much just from looking at it." Longarm patted a coat pocket as if to imply that he had the letter tucked in there. In fact, what he had in that pocket were five excellent-quality cheroots and a rum crook left over from the last time he had had to make do without his favored cheroots.

"Let me have a look at it. Maybe I can figure out where it should go."

"Thanks, but I know where it should go. The postmaster up in Buffalo said I was t' turn it over to the executor of Marshal Franklin's estate. Nobody else. I don't mean t' give offense, but he was real clear about that. So. D'you know who the executor is?"

"Sorry. No."

Longarm thanked the man and ambled on down the street, asking questions about Jim Franklin's estate everywhere he went.

"Shit, there isn't no reason to execute anything," one man snorted. "All old Jim left was a Colt Peacemaker and a sawed-off two-shot shotgun."

"What happened to them?" Longarm asked.

"Damned if I'd know. You might look over there in the marshal's office. They might've been left there for who-ever takes the badge next."

"Thanks. I'll look."

"You do that, mister. Now if you'll excuse me . . ."

Longarm let himself out and headed for the cubbyhole that had been the town marshal's office.

The office damned sure wasn't much. It would have made a fair-sized pantry, nothing more. It held a desk. A swivel chair—that would have been Jim's—and a pair of straight-backed chairs.

Longarm picked up one of the straight chairs and turned it upside down. He smiled. Yeah, this was Jim Franklin's office, all right. The front legs of the straight chair had been sawed short by a half inch or so. Just enough so that someone being questioned would be constantly having to push himself up, would constantly be sliding forward just the least little bit. It was a trick Jim had taught Longarm. Keep the suspect uncomfortable. Keep him on edge. And most of them would not even realize how or why this was happening to them.

Jim's old shotgun was in the rack against the wall— Longarm recognized it instantly—along with a Springfield .50–70 with the Allyn breech-loading conversion. That useless piece of shit was not Jim's. Obviously, it came with the office.

Longarm sat in the swivel chair, the springs creaking loudly when he moved, and checked the desk drawers. There was not much in them. Some paper and ink, a few pens. In the right-hand bottom drawer was Jim's gunbelt carefully rolled around his holster. His .44–40 Colt was still in the holster.

A dark stain on the floor near the desk suggested that this was where Jim died. He had been at or near his desk, obviously not expecting trouble.

Some son of a bitch just walked in and shot Jim down.

Some son of a bitch who Jim did not suspect as a murderer, or that revolver would not have been in the drawer.

"Well, Jim ol' hoss," Longarm whispered, "don't you be fretting none. I'm gonna find whoever done this to you. That's a promise, from me to thee. A promise."

Longarm closed his eyes and sat for long moments before he collected himself and stood.

When he left, he took Jim's Colt and the 12-gauge sawed-off with him.

Chapter 25

Longarm woke up feeling positive about his previous day's work. The seeds had been planted, and with luck they would soon grow . . . into worry for whoever it was who murdered Jim, or hope for whoever sent that telegram. Either way, Longarm figured to pick up some information by way of his lie.

He sat on the edge of his bed and deliberately breathed in and out very deeply for several minutes. He had read an article somewhere that said deep breathing was supposed to be conducive to good health; he had no reason to disbelieve that if a doctor said it was so.

When he was done breathing—so to speak—he poured cold water into the washstand basin and splashed several double handfuls onto his face and neck, snorting like a seal as he did so. Finally, he slicked back his hair, inspected his face in the flake of mirror provided by the hotel, and lighted a cheroot. Only when the cheroot was drawing nicely did he begin getting dressed.

He hesitated for a moment before leaving the room. Hesitated and looked the place over. There was no good place to hide anything, certainly nothing that could be locked. He settled for leaving Jim's revolver and shotgun lying in plain sight. The guns were old and battered, but were clean and oiled. Longarm looked them over again carefully until he was sure he could identify them if need be. Then he closed the room and went to the café for his breakfast.

"You sure know how to warm a man's belly," Longarm told the Mexican when he was finally done stuffing his face.

The Mexican grinned. "It is a shame I am not a woman, no?"

Longarm looked him over from head to toe, then laughed. "No offense, friend, but . . . no. It ain't."

That got a laugh from the café owner, too. Longarm picked up his hat and let himself out into the crisp morning air. He fingered the sharp whisker stubble on his chin, then turned toward the barbershop.

Halfway there, he heard a rush of feet bursting out of an alley. Longarm barely had time enough to whirl around to face the attack.

There were two of them. Young. Muscular. Longarm was certain he had never seen either of them before.

They were armed not with guns but with sand-filled leather coshes.

Longarm could have put an immediate halt to this by simply putting a bullet in the brain of one of them. That would pretty surely discourage the other as well.

But, dammit, that was not the sort of response an ordinary salesman was likely to have. Besides, these young idiots were not armed themselves, and he did not want to give grief to a mother somewhere. Surely hired bullyboys had mothers. Didn't they?

It was not a question to be pondered at the moment, however. Longarm squared off to face them, ducked under a wildly swung cosh, and plunged his fist wrist-deep into that one's gut.

The fellow doubled over clutching his belly, then dropped to his knees and began retching.

The other one came on undeterred. But wary now that his pal was down and puking.

He circled around Longarm like a wolf looking for an opening so it could bring down a deer. Longarm simply stood there, watching and waiting, turning his head but not his body. He figured the kid would come at him when his back was presented.

And he was right.

The fellow jumped in when he was directly behind Longarm, arm raised ready to bring the cosh down on the back of Longarm's skull. A blow like that could cause permanent brain damage. Or worse.

If it landed.

Longarm spun around to face the assault. He stepped into the rush, one arm raised to block the cosh.

The two collided, and Longarm wrenched the heavy leather sap out of the fellow's hand.

"You . . . oh, shit!" His complaint was cut short by Longarm bouncing the cosh off his face. There was a dull crunch of breaking cartilage, and the young fellow's nose was permanently rearranged. Blood spurted and began to flood into his mouth and down his chin and neck. He had to open his mouth in order to breathe, and when he did that he got more blood into it.

"Jesus!" he yelped.

Longarm reached out to grab the fellow's shoulder, but the

cosh he was holding prevented him from getting a good grip. The young man jerked backward, pulling away and stumbling back into the alley he had just come rushing out of.

No harm done, Longarm figured. He could always talk to the other one to find out who sent them.

Except when he turned toward that one, the man bounded to his feet and skedaddled on the heels of his buddy.

"Well, shit," Longarm mumbled. He really would have liked to have a word with those boys. One of them anyway.

Still, he should be pleased enough. It looked like his lie about the undeliverable letter was beginning to pay dividends.

He slipped the cosh into his pocket and resumed his trek to the barbershop.

Chapter 26

"Mornin', Mr. Moore."

"Good morning, Mr. London. Have a seat. I'll be with you in a few minutes."

Longarm nodded and picked up a month-old copy of the *Police Gazette*, which he had read back home in Denver when the articles in it were fresh. Still, having it in front of his face gave him an excuse to sit there with his ears open.

He was hoping someone would rise to the lure he had tossed out about that returned letter. Either that, or the two bullyboys would come to see the barber about their newly acquired ailments and injuries. Longarm was pretty sure there was no doctor in Yesterday, so this would be the logical place for them to seek relief from their hurts.

"Ready for you, Mr. London."

The voice came from far away. He ignored it.

The barber walked over to Longarm and touched his arm. "I said, I'm ready for you, Mr. London."

"Oh. Sorry. I was paying attention t' my reading." The truth was that he hadn't responded because London was not his name. Had Harold Moore invited Custis Long into his chair, Longarm would have heard.

Longarm folded the tabloid and laid it aside. He slipped out of his coat and hung it onto a wall peg, added his gunbelt to the adjoining peg, then took his seat in the barber chair.

"Another trim for you today, Mr. London?"

Longarm shook his head. "Just a shave please, Mr. Moore."

"Yes, sir." Moore made a show of snapping the striped sheet before draping it over Longarm's chest and shoulders. He picked up a razor and began stropping it, the sound of steel striking leather popping loudly. When he was satisfied with the razor, he whipped up a lather in his soap mug and used his thumbs to smooth a very thin sheet of it onto Longarm's cheeks and chin and neck. "There, I think that should do."

Longarm closed his eyes and leaned back against the headrest. He could feel Moore's feathery light touch, could hear the tough whiskers resist as Moore's steel encountered and overcame them.

"Well, lookit this asshole here."

The voice was not one Longarm remembered having heard before. He opened his eyes.

His two young friends from the nearby alley had come in. Through a back door, he noticed. Little bastards probably were not ashamed to show their faces on the public street . . . but they should have been.

"Step aside, Harold. Me and James are gonna beat on this son of a bitch for a spell. Then we may carry him out back an' cut his balls off."

"You'd best not do any such thing," Moore warned. "If you Wickets fuck up one more time, you'll be banned. You know that, George. You know what kind of trouble you got into before. You were told. One more time, and you're out for good."

"I don't think so," George Wicket said.

"Is this his coat over here? It is, ain't it?" James asked. He sidled over beside Longarm's coat and gunbelt. He was grinning when he slid Longarm's double-action .45 Colt from its holster. He turned to face Longarm.

"Not so tough now, are you?" George taunted.

Apparently, it had not occurred to either of the Wickets that the Colt revolver had played no part in their last encounter. The brothers had come at him with coshes. Longarm had not bothered to pull his revolver. Hell, he hadn't needed to.

"Maybe we'll just shoot your ass and take what we want off your dead body, *Mr.* London." James's sneer made the word *mister* sound like a curse word.

"No!" George quickly barked. "He said . . . I mean . . . you shouldn't ought to do that."

"Who said?" Longarm asked. "Who asked you to take that letter from me?"

"Nobody," George answered. He sounded distressed.

Longarm smiled. "That's all right. You don't have t' tell me. I'll work it out by an' by anyhow."

"Dagnabbit, George, I'm gonna shoot this smart-ass son of a bitch," James declared.

"All right, but don't kill him. Just shoot him in, like, his arms or something."

"I won't take easy to the thought of bein' shot," Longarm warned. "An' if I have t' shoot, I won't waste no time trying t' just wound you, James. I'll drill you right in the belly. Right there beside that stain on your shirt. Now I've warned you fair and square, so get the hell out o' here."

"Mister, I'm the one that has the gun here," James snarled. "An' I'm the one is gonna shoot your stupid ass."

Longarm looked at Harold Moore, who was standing by, unhappy but unwilling or unable to do anything about it. "I warned them. You heard me warn them, didn't you, Mr. Moore?"

"I, uh, boys, don't be doing this. You hear me? Don't be doing this shit."

"This is got nothing t' do with you, Mr. Moore, so you just back away."

"Boys . . ." The voice was pleading, but it carried no power.

James Wicket looked down at the Colt revolver in his hand, then used both thumbs to draw the hammer back to firing position.

Longarm's .41-caliber derringer roared, the muzzle flash from it setting Harold Moore's sheet on fire.

A look of sheer amazement came over James Wicket's face. He peered down at the hole in his shirt. The hole was immediately beside an old stain on his shirtfront.

James staggered, managed to right himself, and then crumpled to the floor. George dropped to his knees beside his dying brother.

"If you're reaching for that gun," Longarm said, "you're a dead man."

"I, uh . . . no. I just . . . it's James. You've shot him. He didn't do nothing to you, and you've shot him."

"That's right. He didn't do nothing to me. God knows he tried hard enough, but he wasn't up to the task. Now leave that shooter where it lies an' take your brother."

"Harold. Help him. Please." George looked close to tears.

Tough shit, Longarm thought. He'd warned them. James had made his choices.

Longarm stepped off the barber chair, used the charred sheet to wipe the last of the soap off his face, and retrieved his Colt. "We can finish this some other time," he said to Harold Moore.

"Yes, sir. Right."

Longarm returned the stubby derringer to his vest pocket and let himself out of the barbershop.

Chapter 27

Well, he had certainly spooked *some*-damn-body with that tale about a letter from Jim Franklin to a deputy U.S. marshal. And that somebody had authorized the Wicket boys to damage but not murder the man who was known here as Curtis London. Now just who, he wondered, could that somebody be?

Three guesses. The first two don't count.

There was only one man in Yesterday with that sort of power. His name was Benito Jiggs.

Jiggs could be presumed as well to be the man who had called for Jim Franklin's murder.

The fact that Jim was shot down at his own desk ruled out a panicky response to the town marshal catching someone in the middle of a crime and dying in the line of duty. Had he been found in an alley somewhere or inside a burglarized store, then a more or less accidental death might have been possible. Luck of the draw for a lawman.

But not behind his own desk. Not with his gunbelt stuffed away in a desk drawer and his scattergun standing in the rack.

No, it was clear that Jim had been murdered. Deliberately shot down.

And there was only the one man in Yesterday who could be responsible for that.

Not that Jiggs would have pulled the trigger, if for no other reason than because the man was not likely to get up from his table and walk that far. But he had the power to call for Jim's death.

Longarm wanted the one who had pulled the trigger. Even more than that, he wanted Benito Jiggs's head on a platter.

Longarm's problem, though, or one of them, was that he had no jurisdiction here.

He was not a law enforcement officer of whatever county this was. He was not even Jim Franklin's successor as town marshal. At the moment, Yesterday had no town marshal or any other sort of law that Longarm was aware of. Except for Benito Jiggs. The fat man seemed to be judge and jury in Yesterday. Apportioned out his own brand of ham-handed "justice."

Come to think of it . . .

Longarm stopped practically in mid-stride. He took his time about lighting a cheroot, then pinched it tight between his teeth while he grinned to the busy street before him.

When he was done thinking through the notion that had come to him, he wheeled and headed back the way he had just come, striding past the barbershop and the Mexican's café and on to Mr. Jiggs's handsome casino. Once inside the saloon, he headed straight for the round table where Mr. Jiggs always sat with his cold eyes and sagging jowls.

"You gave me till this evenin' to tell you do I want t' broker for this town," he declared. "Well, I'm ready right now t' tell you what I want to do here."

Jiggs grunted, then said, "When I finish playing this hand. In the meantime, set yourself down and wait for me. No, in that chair right there. Now be quiet, please. I'm trying to concentrate here."

Longarm sat. He was quite content to wait.

Chapter 28

"It occurs to me," Longarm said when Jiggs finally acknowledged him, "that there is a whole lotta opportunity here in Yesterday. You got you what they call a thriving community here. Plenty of money flowing through. No reason why some o' that money shouldn't stick to my fingers." He grinned. "So t' speak."

"Are you saying you do want to accept the position as broker to all these businesses?" Jiggs asked.

"Not exactly," Longarm said, his twisted grin turning sly. He leaned closer and lowered his voice. "There's no town marshal here t' keep order." The grin brightened. "An' collect fines."

"You see opportunity there?" Jiggs asked.

"A world of it," Longarm told him. "For both of us. I figure it t' be on what you call a percentage basis. I rake in the fines an' split the take with you, Mr. Jiggs. The way I see it, this deal should bring you a helluva lot more than the hundred a month I'd be paying as a broker. Better yet, it should put more jingle in my pockets than the brokering ever could."

"What about my boys?" Jiggs nodded toward his ever-present bodyguards.

"What they do is different from what I have in mind," Longarm said.

"True. True." Jiggs nibbled slowly at a fingernail that was already bitten down to the quick. After a few moments of that, he looked at Longarm again. "I see the logic of your position, Mr. London. What do you need from me to make it happen?"

"Just a badge an' your authority t' use it."

Jiggs thought some more, then grunted and said, "All right. I will have the badge brought to you."

"Thank you, Mr. Jiggs. You won't regret this." That, Longarm figured, was a bald-faced lie. Jiggs was damned sure going to regret this decision. Custis Long intended to see to it.

Jiggs was conferring with the bodyguards before Longarm reached the door on his way out.

Longarm was having lunch in the café when one of the bodyguards came in. Men who were standing in the doorway waiting for chairs to become available moved aside when the tall, heavily built bodyguard moved through. The three who were already seated at the same table as Longarm picked up their bowls of stew and carried them to the side of the tiny café, where they proceeded to eat standing up. Longarm simply watched the approach of the bodyguard.

The man helped himself to one of the newly vacated chairs. No one else came forward to occupy the others.

"My name is Homer Livingston," he said, reaching into a coat pocket. "Anything you want, you come to me about it. Don't bother Mr. Jiggs with the nitpicky shit. And don't try to hold out on him. You do that, me and my partner Freddy will come talk to you. Trust me. You wouldn't like

112

what we would say nor how we would say it." He brought his hand out and held a closed fist over the table. When he opened his fingers, a round metal disk dropped onto the table with a muted clang. A star shape was etched onto the surface with one word, "Marshal."

Longarm smiled when he saw that. Mr. Jiggs and his asshole companions had no idea how accurate the description was. Longarm picked up the badge, examined it for a moment, and pinned it onto his coat.

"There. Now you're official," Livingston said.

Longarm chuckled.

"Is there anything you need from me?"

Longarm shook his head. "Nothing I can think of right at this minute."

"If there is, you know where to find me." Livingston started to rise, but Longarm stopped him with a light touch on the sleeve.

"Yeah?"

"One thing," Longarm said. "The last fella that wore this badge. I heard he was shot. What was that all about?"

"Franklin was a nice man but maybe too nice, if you know what I mean. Thought he ought to do things his way. For most things that's all right, but you don't want to be doing anything contrary to what the boss wants. Marshal Franklin didn't understand that."

"What was his mistake exactly?"

Livingston shook his head. "You don't need to know that." He stood and walked away without a backward glance.

There was something in the way Homer Livingston carried himself that suggested he might know how to use his gun, might even use it effectively and often, but that he really preferred to use his own powerful fists to batter an opponent into submission.

The other one—Livingston had called him Freddy—was probably cut from the same cloth.

Longarm went back to his meal, and soon the vacant chairs at his table were filled.

Chapter 29

"Hello, Sam."

The storekeeper did a double take when he spotted the badge pinned to Longarm's lapel. "Are you really a marshal?" The man sounded hopeful.

"Ayuh, I am now. I'm the new town marshal."

"Oh, for a minute there, I thought . . ." Pendergast shook his head and shuddered. "For just a minute, I thought you might be something else. My mistake."

"What did you think I might be, Sam?"

"It doesn't matter."

"Maybe not. There's something I want t' talk to you about, Sam. Now that I've took this badge, I want to look into a murder that happened here in Yesterday. I want t' look into the shooting of Marshal Jim Franklin."

"You might best leave that question be, Mr. London."

"Why is that, Mr. Pendergast?"

The aging storekeeper only shook his head.

"Lookahere," Longarm said, "you been here longer'n anybody. Since before Yesterday *was* a town, if I understand it right."

"That's true, but what is your point?"

"I figure you should know more about Yesterday—an' what goes on here—than anybody. Might even be that you know something about Jim Franklin's murder."

"Why should you care about that, Mr. London? It happened before you ever saw our little community. Marshal Franklin's death shouldn't affect you."

"It's a murder. Nobody's been charged for it. I'd like to solve it. Put the killer behind bars."

"I guess you haven't noticed then. Yesterday has no jail. There is no place here to lock someone up."

"What happens if somebody's arrested?" Longarm asked, genuinely curious.

"There are only two punishments. Fines and banishment."

"Banishment?"

"That is when—"

"Oh, I know what the word means, but that doesn't seem like much of a punishment."

"You don't understand the sort of people who trade in this community, do you?"

"I'm beginnin' to think that maybe I don't," Longarm admitted. "I'd appreciate it if you'd explain."

"I . . . I don't know," Pendergast said. He stood there behind his counter, indecisive, until a customer came in, a tall, muscular man who looked vaguely familiar to Longarm. The storekeeper turned away and ignored Longarm while he waited on the customer. When he was done with the transaction, he no longer seemed inclined to speak.

"Maybe we can talk about this later," Longarm suggested.

Pendergast only grunted in response.

Chapter 30

It was Longarm's experience that if you wanted to find out the down and dirty of a place, any place, there were two likely spots to start looking. One of those was a barbershop. The other was a whorehouse.

Under Mr. Jiggs's rules, there would be only one whorehouse in Yesterday, but Longarm had never been there. He was of the opinion that newly appointed Town Marshal Curtis London ought to drop by and get acquainted. He stopped in at the gentlemen's haberdasher's to ask directions.

He couldn't miss it. The town pleasure palace was a rambling, two-story affair that was painted white—not merely whitewashed but coated thick with real, lead-based wall paint—and trimmed in red. A pair of lamps with red glass panels hung on either side of the door, unlighted at this late daylight hour. Longarm mounted the front porch, then carefully wiped his boots and removed his hat before he gave the bellpull a tug. Somewhere inside, he heard a faint jangle to announce his call.

The door was opened a minute or two later—it seemed longer—by a woman with henna-red hair and the prominent

117

veins of old age. "You'll have to come back in a couple hours, honey. We ain't open yet."

"That's all right," Longarm said, smiling. "I just want to talk. T' get acquainted, sort of."

"Why would I want to get acquainted with you, mister?"

Longarm realized that he happened to be holding his hat against his chest where it blocked the sight of his badge. He dropped his hand to his side, and the old madam snorted. "Found them another one, have they? I hope to hell you're more agreeable than that last one was."

Jim had given her trouble? That was interesting. It was the first Longarm had heard about it.

"That's the sort of thing I came here t' talk to you about," Longarm smoothly lied. "I'd like t' come inside now an' sit down. Have a cup o' coffee or somethin' to drink. I'd like t' go over your expectations of me and then, if necessary, I'll tell you what I expect of you."

"All right, Marshal London. Come in."

"So you do know my name," Longarm said.

"Knew the name already, but wasn't familiar with the face to go with it. Now I am." She stepped back from the door, and Longarm went inside.

The place was nicely appointed with the customary heavy draperies and flocked wallpaper. A sitting room filled with upholstered furniture was on one side of the house, and a huge parlor on the other. There was a staircase in the center. Presumably, that was where the girls would be.

"My name is Miss Margarite," the madam said.

"I presume you work for Mr. Jiggs, just like all the rest of us."

Margarite did not respond to that. She did turn and ask, "Would you like to sit in the parlor here?"

"I can hear a bunch o' ladies' voices comin' from the back. I'd kinda like to meet them if you don't mind."

"My girls—there are eight of them—are having breakfast. They will pretty themselves up when they're done eating. You might be more favorably impressed if you meet them when they have their makeup in place and their nice gowns on."

"I would prefer meeting them now if you don't mind," he said.

Margarite shrugged. "Suit yourself. Just don't expect much." She started toward the back of the house, toward the kitchen. "By the way, you being our town marshal won't get you any free fucks. I can give you a discount. Fifty cents instead of the usual dollar. But the girl will still have to get her share. Mr. Jiggs will forgo his cut, but it wouldn't be fair to the girls for them to lose out."

"Thanks for telling me." At the moment, Longarm was just about broke. He doubted he could afford a fifty-cent piece of ass even if he wanted to pay for it. Hell, he was worried about being able to pay for his next meal, never mind buying pussy.

The kitchen Margarite led him to was large, with a long table in the middle of the room and a pair of wood-fired ranges against the back wall. There were seven girls gathered around the table like so many pigeons fluttering and squawking after some spilled birdseed.

A tall, cadaverous man was standing over the stoves. He seemed to be doing his best to ignore the women. They, in turn, were ignoring him.

Longarm was not impressed by the quality of the whores. Every one of them had flyaway hair in wild disarray. They wore faded, ratty housecoats with damned little under them. Most wore old carpet slippers, but two were barefoot.

Longarm had seen prettier women than these in his last nightmare. But he would have wagered that these could present a brave show once they were washed and made up and properly dressed.

It is a funny thing, but men pretty much are the way they are going to be no matter their circumstances. Women, on the other hand, can go from butt ugly to ravingly gorgeous at the stroke of a comb and a rouge pot.

These . . . they were in critical need of that comb and rouge pot.

"Ladies. Give me your attention. Is everyone here? No? Who is missing. Betty? Is she still with her gentleman?"

"Yes, Miz Margarite."

The madam shifted her attention to the cook, who must have been something more than just a cook. "What about it, Bill? Is the gentleman paid for tonight?"

The tall man shook his head. "Paid up through last night, but no longer'n that."

"Aggie, run upstairs and tell Betty that her gentleman has to leave. Right now. Either that or pay for another night." She turned to Longarm and said, "All night is three dollars. No exceptions. He knows that. So does she." She raised her voice and added, "Ladies, this is Marshal London. I want you to make him feel that he is among friends here."

"That's mighty nice o' all of you," Longarm said.

"Come over here, Marshal London. Sit beside me. Would you like some breakfast?" The girl issuing the invitation was blond and busty. She looked used up even though she was probably not yet out of her twenties.

"Thank you, miss. I've already et, but I could enjoy a cup o' coffee."

120

"I'll get it for him," a little brunette chirped, jumping up from her chair and scurrying to the nearer stove.

Within moments, Longarm was comfortably seated with a cup of steaming coffee in front of him and a bevy of women surrounding him.

He was on his second cup when two women and a muscular, heavyset man walked into the room.

The man immediately blurted, "You!" and went for his pistol.

Chapter 31

Longarm leaped up, his Colt clearing leather as he did so. The man in the doorway shoved one of the whores out of his way and raised his pistol.

Longarm's Colt spat first, a heavy lead slug crashing into the side of the gunman's face. The bullet ripped through bone and blood, tearing away most of the man's jaw and severing his carotid artery on its way through.

The man spun halfway around, just in time for Longarm's second shot to shatter his left temple and turn his brain into mush. He dropped to the floor like a marionette with its strings cut, his revolver firing reflexively.

One of the whores screamed.

Then the rest did as well. But the first kept it up, clutching her leg and moaning that she was shot.

The truth was that she indeed was shot. The gunman's errant bullet had lodged in her upper thigh. A fountain of blood squirted out of her torn flesh with every beat of her heart.

Longarm grabbed a linen napkin and stuffed it into the wound to stanch the bleeding. The whore shrieked anew at that excruciating pain, but the woman would die if she continued to bleed.

"Is there a doctor in town?" he asked.

Margarite shook her head. "Just the barber."

"Get him. This has t' be tended to." He grabbed the nearest girl by the elbow. "You. Go get him. Tell him t' bring his medical kit. Tell him why. He'll know what t' do better'n me."

Longarm turned his attention to the madam. "What the hell was that all about? Who was he? Why'd he draw on me like that?"

The truth was that Longarm already knew the answers to all those questions.

The son of a bitch drew because he recognized Longarm as a federal deputy and thought—incorrectly as it happened—that Custis Long was here to arrest him for robbery of the mail.

The newly dead fellow's name was Jeremy Taylor and he was wanted on warrants out of Idaho, Colorado, and Kansas. And those were just charges that Longarm happened to know about.

He shouted and dragged iron when he recognized Longarm. It was just a stroke of luck that the man hadn't blurted Longarm's real name when he saw him.

Margarite sniffed. "It's just a damn good thing the bastard didn't die owing us money." She did not seem shaken up by the sudden demise of one of her customers.

"He called himself Jerry Tyler," she said. "He came here to blow off steam after a robbery over in Idaho. Everyone told him this is a safe place. No one would bother him here. He probably panicked when he saw your badge," she said.

"Bill, Marshal London, both of you help me get Linda upstairs, will you? Girls, you help, too. Ginny, I want you to clean up all this blood. Aggie, I want you to stand at the door. As soon as Mr. Moore gets here, bring him upstairs. Go on now. Everybody get to it."

With Margarite directing everyone else—and getting in the way while she did it—the two men and five whores managed to drag the howling, weeping whore up the narrow stairs and onto her rumpled, sweat-stinking bed.

They dumped her on the bed. Then Longarm and the man called Bill went back downstairs. The girls and Margarite stayed with their fallen comrade.

"Is she all right?" Aggie asked as they reached the bottom of the stairs.

"She will be," Bill told her. To Longarm he said, "Care for a fresh cup of coffee?"

"No, thanks. I'd best go in town and walk my rounds. I have a lot to learn. Let me ask you something, though. This place—the town I mean—is there something I should be knowing about it? Something sort of—odd?"

Bill chuckled. But he did not come right out and actually say anything.

Chapter 32

The next morning, Longarm was in Harold Moore's barber chair, half his face covered in lather and a straight razor to his throat, when a man he did not know—but who looked familiar from a wanted poster—came into the little shop.

Cletus Murphy, he realized after a moment's thought. Wanted for bank robbery down in Nebraska. Of course Curtis London, a simple commodities broker, was not supposed to know that.

"Are you Marshal London?" Murphy asked.

Longarm nodded.

"Mr. Jiggs wants to see you."

"All right. You can tell him I'll be over quick as I finish my shave here, an' I thank you for the message."

"No, mister, you don't understand. Mr. Jiggs don't ask to see people *later*. If he calls for somebody, he wants to see him *now*."

Longarm smiled. "When I'm done here."

Moore began unpinning the sheet. "We can finish this later, Marshal."

"Perhaps I didn't make myself clear. I'm in the middle o' something here. I'll go see Mr. Jiggs when I'm done."

"Yes, sir." Moore's hand was not nearly as steady with the blade after that, though, and the splash of bay rum afterward made several fresh nicks sting.

True to his word, Longarm collected his gunbelt, coat, and hat and ambled over to the casino when he left the barbershop. He paid with a coin pilfered off the body of Jeremy Taylor the day before—not that the son of a bitch had much on him when he died, damn him.

"You wanted to see me?"

Jiggs was at his usual table, surrounded by a different set of cronies, who moved away when Longarm sat down to discuss business with the boss.

"Something to eat? A drink maybe?" Jiggs offered.

"I'm fine, thanks. Already had breakfast at the café, an' it's a mite early for whiskey."

Jiggs nodded. "Good. I didn't think you were a lush. This proves it."

"That was easy." Longarm smiled and started to rise.

"Oh, sit your ass down there. We got to go over some rules, you and me," Mr. Jiggs said. "Otherwise, you could end up shooting me out of business here."

Longarm settled back onto his chair. "Now I'm confused," he said.

"Yesterday you killed one of this town's good customers." Mr. Jiggs waved his pudgy hand, the fat on it so puffy that his knuckles had pretty well disappeared. "Not that I am faulting you," he quickly added. "The man saw your badge and went for his gun. It was just your good fortune that you shot him first. I understand that, and I would never ask a man to give his life for me. Especially not for mere profit. But I want to make it clear that I do not really condone the shooting of our"—he smiled—"clients."

"Clients," Longarm repeated slowly. "I think maybe I don't understand."

"It is simple enough," Mr. Jiggs said. "The town of Yesterday thrives on trade from men who are, how shall I put this? They are wanted for crimes committed elsewhere. They are safe here. They spend their money here. They know not to cause any real trouble in Yesterday. If they do, they are warned. There is no second warning. They are banned. Banished, if you will. None of them wants that, believe me. That is why your job should be simple enough. You ride herd on the drunks. Stop any fights. Come and tell me if there are serious problems."

"An' if some simple-minded sonuvabitch draws down on me?"

"In that case, I have no quarrel with you shooting him. You did the right thing yesterday, Mr. London. Please understand that. I just wanted you to . . . more fully understand the rules we live by here."

"I think you've cleared things up nicely," Longarm said. "May I ask you something?"

"Of course."

"The fella that wore this badge before me. D'you think he had the same sort o' situation? One o' your guests seeing the badge an' reacting badly?"

"That is not something we are ever likely to know, is it," Mr. Jiggs responded. "The old man is dead and buried, and no one knows who killed him. Or why."

Not yet, they don't, Longarm thought silently to himself. But he damn well still intended to find out.

Mr. Jiggs motioned for the hangers-on to return, indicating that Longarm's audience with the great man was at an end. Longarm stood. "Thank you, sir. I appreciate what you've told me here. It clears up a lot."

"I'm glad to be able to do it," Mr. Jiggs said. "If you change your mind about having that meal or something to eat, just tell them at the bar over there. In fact, you will find that you don't need to pay for food or drink or your hotel room. Not from now on. And don't worry. You will not be embarrassed with a bill for any such services. Everyone has been told. You are one of my people now."

"Thank you," Longarm said again, trying his best to be the meekly obsequious little civil servant. "Thank you."

He turned tail and headed for the door. Quick, lest he puke at having to kowtow even one moment longer to that fat, ugly bastard Jiggs.

Chapter 33

"Wait a minute, can't you?" Glenda Bateman came hurrying out of a side room in a swirl of skirts. She laid her fingertips on Longarm's forearm and smiled up at him. "Please."

Longarm glanced back toward Mr. Jiggs. At their table nearby, Homer Livingston and the bodyguard named Freddy were already on their feet, as if sensing trouble ahead. Longarm believed he could take them—the day he failed to believe that was the day he ought to get out of the business—but he hoped like hell he would not have to prove that.

"Please," Glenda repeated. She tugged him back toward Mrs. Jiggs's table.

"Benny," she whined when they got there, "I'm bored, and Marshal London is the only friend I have in Yesterday, except for you, honey. Would it be all right with you for Marshal London to take me down the street for an ice cream? You know I simply dote on ice cream, Benny, honey, and I'm wanting some this morning. Please?" Longarm thought she sounded like a little kid trying to wheedle permission to go get a candy.

Livingston and Freddy both settled back into their chairs and their ever-present card game.

"Sure, darlin'," Mr. Jiggs responded in his deep, bull-frog voice. "You run on and get you some ice cream. Curtis, you take care of this little lady. Get her whatever she wants. Remember, though. There won't nobody charge you for anything. If they try to, you tell me about it when you get back, you hear?"

"Yes, sir, Mr. Jiggs. I'll take good care of her."

"I know you will, son. I know you will." But it was obvious that Mr. Jiggs's attention was back on the cards in his hand.

Longarm offered his arm to Glenda and led her out of the casino. The bodyguards ignored them.

"Are you all right?" he asked when they were outside with no one else around to hear.

Glenda giggled. "It went like a charm, Custis."

"Curtis," he corrected her. "I wouldn't want t' confuse anyone."

"Oh, all right. But I think it is awfully funny, the famous lawman Longarm playing at being a town marshal in little bitty old Yesterday where nothing ever happens."

Longarm was not so sure he would agree that nothing ever happened in Yesterday. But he did not want to stand there and argue the point with her. "You say he bought your virgin act?" he asked, returning to his original question. The truth was that he had been wondering about it. Now was his chance to find out.

"Of course he did, darlin'." She giggled. "Though we had us a just *awful* time trying to get me laid. You see—and you might not know this, darlin', fat men's peckers is anchored in place. They pile up fat and it makes their hard-ons shorter. Mr. Jiggs, he only has about two, two and a half inches left to work with. Though come to think of it, darlin', if he was to lose that belly he would have a fine pole there, I'm thinking.

"Anyway, with that little bitty ol' thing and all that fat to get around, we had us a terrible time trying to pop my cherry. We got it done, but it took some sweat and strain, let me tell you." Glenda giggled.

"What I'm hoping is that he'll let me just suck him off from now on. I don't mind that. Hell, it's what I've been doing for a living since I was a little kid anyway. And he's real easy to get off. That little cock just squirts and squirts, darlin'. In here is the ice cream. They had wild strawberry yesterday." She giggled. "Yesterday in Yesterday. Isn't that funny, darlin'?" Glenda led Longarm into the tiny ice cream parlor, her face lighting up with childish glee at the prospect of an ice cream.

She got her strawberry confection and carried it outside. "I want you to do something for me," she said.

"Name it."

"I want to feel a proper dick inside me for a change. I want you to fuck me again."

"Don't you think that might be a little dangerous?" Longarm asked.

Glenda giggled. "Of course I do, darlin'. Of *course* I do!"

Chapter 34

The girl was nothing if not inventive. First standing up against a bridge railing. Next as a virgin. Now she wanted it in the alley beside the ice cream shop. She even kept her grip on her ice cream and as far as Longarm could see, didn't spill a drop.

He, on the other hand, spilled a load. A hot load.

Glenda led him into the alley—in broad daylight—and leaned against the wall. She lifted the front of her dress and used the voluminous mass of cloth and crinolines to hide Longarm's pecker, which she quite happily released from the imprisonment of his fly.

"Oh, darlin'. That's better," she said when it slid inside her body. Her no-longer-virgin body. "Now, hold still for a minute there, darlin'." Glenda ground her hips against him. Then she stopped.

"I have an idea," she said.

"I shudder t' think what it might be, but . . . what's your idea?" Longarm asked.

"You're the sheriff now, right?"

"Wrong."

"You aren't?"

"I'm the town marshal," he said.

"What is the difference?" She sounded genuinely interested, so he told her.

"A sheriff, dear girl, is the law officer for an entire county. A town marshal's jurisdiction stops at the town limits."

"What about what you really are?" she asked.

"A deputy United States marshal has jurisdiction everywhere in the country," he said. "But only for crimes involving United States law and when local law officers request help from us. Which hasn't happened here, which is why I'm acting on my own here." He waggled his hips from side to side. "And what could any o' this have t' do with your suggestion, whatever it is?"

Glenda giggled. "I was just thinking. I've never done it in a jail cell."

"And you ain't gonna do it in one now neither. Turns out that Yesterday don't have a proper jail."

"What about the marshal's office?" she asked.

"There's an office but no cells in it."

"Then can't we do it in the marshal's office? Please?"

As foolishly dangerous as that sounded to him, it was not half as dumb as standing against a wall ten feet off the public street in broad daylight.

Longarm pulled his pecker out, the air chill on his flesh, wet from hers, and allowed Glenda to tuck him in and button him up again.

The girl returned her dish of melting ice cream to the parlor owner, and walked with Longarm to the town marshal's office. There he shut and latched the door, but knew better than to lower the blinds. That would only call attention to the place.

"I want to get naked," Glenda said.

"No!" Longarm blurted. "Don't be doin' that."

"Why? If anyone comes in we'll be caught anyway." She began removing her clothes.

Longarm groaned. Damn the girl. She had no sense whatsoever. And it made it all the worse for him to realize that she was right. If anyone came in, they were dead ducks anyway, so what did it matter whether Glenda was properly clothed or not?

In for a penny, in for a pound. Wasn't that the old saying?

Longarm began stripping off his coat and vest.

"Darlin', darlin'," Glenda whispered after the second time they both came. She snuggled against his chest and sighed.

Then she straightened and became suddenly brisk and businesslike.

"What's up here?" Longarm asked.

"I've spent too long having that ice cream," Glenda said. "I need to get back to Benny before he gets upset with me." She shuddered. "If he was to get really mad, I don't know what he might do. Benny is a very dangerous man, you know."

"He is? Why d'you say that?"

"Benny has had men killed."

"He told you that?"

Glenda nodded, her expression worried.

"Who?"

"I don't know who exactly, but he told me he had somebody killed here just a couple weeks ago."

Jim Franklin? It could be. The time was certainly right.

It could well be that it was Benito Jiggs who ordered the murder of the last town marshal. Homer Livingston and his buddy Freddy would likely be willing to murder at their boss's command. But why would Jiggs do that when Jim Franklin presumably was his own employee?

Surely, Jim had known when he took the position that Yesterday was a safe haven for outlaws and scoundrels looking for a place to blow off steam and spend some of their ill-gotten profits.

Or had he? Longarm had known something was rotten here when he agreed to take the job, but he had not known exactly what the scam was. He'd only learned that after the fact. Jim might well have had the same experience.

That would explain the murder. Jim might well have been killed so he could not call in Longarm and the other deputies to clean out this nest of snakes.

Thinking about his dead friend, Longarm scarcely noticed when Glenda Bateman finished dressing and hurried out onto the street.

Longarm stayed behind in the office that had been Jim's.

Chapter 35

Longarm sat at the desk that had been Jim Franklin's and thought about what he needed to do next. The situation was simple enough. Benito Jiggs had created an island of lawlessness right in the middle of Wyoming Territory.

The man had even created his own law enforcement here by way of a tame town marshal. Or so he thought.

As long as the county left him alone—or, more likely, did not know about him—he was safe from any form of outside law.

With an exception. A rather important exception.

Since Wyoming was not a state, federal law had leeway to operate here that would not be permissible elsewhere in the country. And Longarm intended to take advantage of that now.

Custis Long intended to put the brakes on Benito Jiggs's scheme. He intended to send a wire to Billy Vail. With the information Longarm provided, Billy could get a federal judge to sign warrants for the arrest of Jiggs and the dispersal of his miniature empire here.

Longarm pulled open the desk that had been his mentor's before him. He found a pencil and paper and jotted down the main points he wanted to include in his wire to Billy, then folded the paper and shoved it in a pocket.

He left the town marshal's office and walked up to the livery, where he hitched the little mare to his rented buggy. The liveryman made no mention of payment this time. But then Marshal London worked for Mr. Jiggs . . . didn't he?

Longarm climbed onto the seat. He could not help remembering the last time he used this rig. Glenda was beside him then. He wished like hell that she was again now, not because he wanted to fuck her again but because he was worried about her safety. There was no telling what Jiggs would demand of her next.

Just looking at Jiggs gave Longarm the impression that being with him would be enough to gag a goat. He suspected that Glenda was skating on thin ice by staying with that son of a bitch.

Still, there was no reasonable excuse Longarm could use to get her away from the man.

He released the brake on the buggy, snapped the driving whip to get the mare's attention, and set off on the road out of Yesterday.

Longarm camped that night in a grove of cottonwood and willow trees. He would have been more comfortable if he had brought some food along, but he had not wanted to tip his hand and show that he intended to be gone for a while.

As it was, he was uncertain whether he should return to Yesterday or wait in Buffalo for whoever Billy sent up to help him clean up the town.

As it was, he really did not have to worry about waiting for the boys. When he woke up the following morning, Homer Livingston and Freddy were there.

Chapter 36

"Good morning. Would you, uh, mind pointing that thing someplace else," Longarm drawled from his makeshift bed on the buggy seat. Freddy was holding a very large-gauge double-barrel shotgun, and the gaping tubes were aimed roughly at Longarm's gut. All it would take would be a slight squeeze of Freddy's finger, and . . .

He sat up and acted meek as a kitten while Livingston collected his gunbelt and—dammit—his derringer, too. That was the problem with a trick like the derringer. Use it once, as he had in the barbershop the other day, and every-damn-body knew about it afterward.

Freddy's attention never wavered and the shotgun barrels scarcely moved. At this close range, even the lightest bird shot would rip a man in two. Longarm shuddered to think what a load of buck could do.

"I take it there's something you fellas want?" Longarm asked. "Is it robbery you have in mind? Want me t' cook you some breakfast? Just tell me. We can figure this out."

Neither Freddy nor Homer Livingston spoke until Longarm's weapons had been collected, their horses brought up from a nearby copse, and Longarm's guns tucked away in their saddlebags. Only then did Homer say, "If you want to take a shit or a leak, go ahead. We're going to be traveling for half the day, so make yourself comfortable. And mind you, me and Freddy got nothing personal against you. This is just a job to us. But we'll blow your ass apart if you try and fuck with us. Believe it."

Longarm believed it.

The two stood watch over him while Longarm took a piss, then gathered up the harness and fitted it onto the mare. That was a chore he was becoming more adept at from repeated use. He hitched the mare to the buggy, then stood waiting for instruction.

Homer nodded, acknowledging Longarm's docile behavior, and said, "Go ahead. Get on. We'll be right behind you."

"Where are we going?"

"You know good and well where we're taking you."

Longarm shrugged. Back to Yesterday, it seemed. Without a stop in Buffalo to send that telegram. Dammit.

As far as Billy Vail and the other deputies knew, Longarm was taking some personal time. They knew where he was but not why, and they had no reason to ask.

The simple truth was . . . he was on his own here.

Chapter 37

"No, don't go to the livery. We'll get somebody to take care of the buggy. You just drive to the casino. That's fine. Now stay where you are until I step down and have my gun on you. Fine. All right, Freddy, I've got him. You can get down now."

Homer knew what he was doing. There was no moment of inattention. Longarm's show of docile obedience gained him nothing.

This was *not* going the way he might have hoped.

Benito Jiggs's boys were professionals, damn them.

"Inside now. Nice and slow."

Jiggs was missing from his usual table. Instead of taking Longarm there, Homer and Freddy led him through a hallway and into a small, windowless room that he judged would be at the far back corner of the casino building.

Lamplight burning bright showed an ugly scene inside the room. Glenda Bateman was there, her wrists captured in thick handcuffs that were chained high on a wall. She was naked and had been badly beaten. Whip marks crisscrossed on her breasts and belly, and her pubic hair had been burned away with a candle or some other open flame.

Blisters on her breasts and nipples suggested she had been burned there, too.

Jiggs sat slouched in a sturdy chair in front of her, the coils of a blacksnake whip lying across his lap. The fat man smiled gleefully when he saw Longarm.

"Marshal!" he said, as if surprised by the visit. "How nice of you to drop by. Miss Bateman here has been telling me about you . . . Marshal *Long*!"

Jiggs shook his head sadly. "Custis Long. Curtis London. Surely, you could have done better than that."

"It was a spur-o'-the-moment thing," Longarm said. "I hadn't actually planned t' be somebody else." He grinned. "But it seemed a good idea at the time."

"At the time. Yes." Jiggs chuckled. "Lucky for me my lovely little friend here decided to tell the whole truth. Did you know that she was not the pure and innocent little virgin she pretended to be? Oh, yes. It's true. But she has confessed now. She has told me pretty much everything she knows."

The whip he had been holding lashed out, the tail of the blacksnake hissing through the air until it loudly cracked on Glenda's unprotected right breast.

The girl screamed. Tears streamed down her cheeks and snot ran from what was left of her nose.

"Did you know," Jiggs said in an amused, conversational tone of voice, "that dear Glenda's real name is Sally? It's true. Sally Carruthers. From Metairie, Louisiana. She tells me she always thought Glenda was a classy name. And she didn't want her family to be shamed by her whoring. Isn't that interesting."

The whip cracked again and Glenda—or Sally—passed out, her slender form hanging limp from the chains that bound her.

Jiggs ponderously turned his chair around so he could face Longarm. "There is room on that wall for one more," he said. "Or would you rather tell me what I want to know?"

"That kinda depends on what you have in mind," Longarm said.

"I want to know why you are here, of course. Who sent you. What you have reported back to your superiors." Jiggs smiled, the expression darkly evil on his fat face. "I want to know . . . everything."

"You know good an' well who would've sent me. I'm a deputy United States marshal. I work for U.S. Marshal William Vail. He's in charge o' the Denver office. Which is where I come from. As fer why, you know that as good as I do. You're on United States soil here. The laws o' this country apply, with or without territorial approval, with or without local consent."

"Interesting, but I don't believe I have broken any federal laws," Jiggs said. "I try to be careful about such things."

"In that case, you got nothing t' worry about." Longarm turned toward Homer and Freddy, who were still standing behind him. "Hand me back my guns, boys, an' step outa my way."

Both bodyguards looked to their boss for instruction. Longarm had no doubt that either of them would have pulled a trigger on him without a moment's hesitation.

He acted more quickly than they.

Longarm jumped not for the door, which they might have expected, but farther into the room.

He leaped behind Jiggs and snatched the blacksnake out of his hands.

Longarm took a quick wrap of the slender whip around Jiggs's fleshy neck and pulled it tight, cutting off the big man's airway.

145

Jiggs began to turn red. Then purple.

He croaked hoarsely. He bleated. He pounded the arm of the chair he was sitting in.

"Your boss is a dead man if I tug just the least little bit more," Longarm warned. "Now lay down your guns and get the hell outa here. Him an' me an' that girl there are going for a little drive, and I'll expect you t' stand aside an' leave be."

He said it as if he expected to be obeyed. Perhaps that made the difference. To his utter amazement, both Homer and Freddy carefully placed their weapons on the floor and backed out of the room.

Longarm felt somewhat better when they were gone.

He still, however, had the small problem of how to get himself and Glenda—Sally—away from Yesterday without either of them getting shot.

Chapter 38

"All right, you fat tub o' shit," Longarm said when the room was clear. "I want you t' set real still while I check t' see do you have any weapons on you."

He frisked Jiggs carefully, then made him remove his shoes and roll up his pants legs to make sure he was not hiding any weapons there. "Now stand up."

"I can't. I need help," Jiggs said.

"It's your choice, but if you don't stand up, I intend t' use this whip on you till you do."

Jiggs practically jumped to his feet.

"I think the word for that is incentive," Longarm mumbled aloud.

Keeping a close eye on Benito Jiggs, Longarm backed toward the door, knelt, and retrieved the guns Homer and Freddy had been nice enough to leave there for him. He stuffed their revolvers, one a Colt and the other a Smith and Wesson Schofield, into his waistband. He snapped open the breech of the double gun and checked the loads—No. 2 duck shot, heavy enough to rip a man to pieces at close range—before closing it again.

Longarm cocked the shotgun. Jiggs was watching him

closely. Which was exactly what Longarm wanted. He wanted the son of a bitch to know that he had checked to make sure the shotgun was loaded and cocked.

"Now unlock those cuffs and lift the girl down," he ordered. "Carefully."

"I don't have the key."

"Then you'd best be damned quick to pick those locks 'cause the only use I got for you is t' carry her out o' here. If I have t' go on my own, I'll leave you dead on this floor right here."

Jiggs was visibly sweating. "Maybe, I . . . uh, maybe I can find the key."

"You do that, Benny. You just go ahead an' do that."

Jiggs took a key from his right-hand coat pocket and unlocked both handcuffs. The battered and bloody girl sagged against him.

"Pick her up."

"I can't. She's too heavy."

"What did I tell you about needin' you, Benny?" Longarm gestured with the tubes of the shotgun. "That girl is the only thing keepin' you alive, Benny. I suggest you treat her real nice."

"Yes. Of course."

Jiggs picked Glenda up in his arms, seemingly with no difficulty at all. The man was fat, but there was a lot of muscle under there, too. Longarm reminded himself to keep that in mind and not take Jiggs for granted.

"Set Glenda in that chair for a second," Longarm ordered.

Jiggs complied.

"Now take off your coat an' wrap it around her. I don't want a bunch o' strangers staring at her naked and hurt."

"She doesn't—"

"Not a word," Longarm snapped. "Not one fucking word. Just do it."

Jiggs did as Longarm instructed.

"Fine. Now pick her up. Careful. Now what we are gonna do, Benny, is that you are gonna carry the girl, an' me, I'll be marching right at your back with this shotgun ready t' go off should any sonuvabitch try an' shoot me or something. Do we understand each other, Benny? Well, do we?" Longarm nudged the back of the man's head with the muzzles of the double-barrel. Jiggs cringed. And nodded.

"Good," Longarm said. "Now real slow an' easy, let's go out to the buggy that's parked out front."

"This position is awkward. May I shift her to a more comfortable one?"

"Go ahead. Be as brave as you like when you do it, but if I think you're up to something, I'll go ahead an' shoot and worry about getting clear afterward."

"No tricks. I am . . . I'm not that brave."

"Somehow, I didn't think so. Go on now. Slow."

The three of them, Glenda being carried by Jiggs and Longarm tucked in close behind, left the room and returned to the casino floor. The casino was silent. It had been emptied of customers and now only Homer Livingston and Freddy—Longarm still did not know that asshole's last name—were visible. Both of them had their hands empty.

"If you follow us, your boss dies," Longarm said, "an' if your boss dies, there won't be anybody t' pay your wages, boys. But you do what you think is best, you hear?"

Neither of the bodyguards said anything.

Jiggs carried the girl out into the street where the mare and buggy stood waiting. Longarm was damned glad now that they had not taken the time earlier to unhitch.

There was not room for the three of them in the light buggy, not when one of them was as large as Jiggs.

"Lay Glenda in the luggage boot," he ordered.

"Her name is Sally," Jiggs said, as if that mattered at this moment.

"She's Glenda to me. Now do what I told you. Put her on the boot there."

Jiggs very carefully placed Glenda—Sally—on the shelf intended for luggage. He adjusted the coat more closely around her.

Longarm stepped half a pace back. "Good. Now climb in."

Jiggs offered no argument. He climbed onto the buggy, one side sagging on the springs when he did so. Lord only knows what the big man weighed.

Longarm walked around to the front of the rig and unclipped the hitch weight, tossed it onto the floor of the buggy, and climbed in. He was delighted to see that his own gunbelt and derringer were lying on the floor of the buggy.

"Turn," he said, reaching into his coat pocket.

"Why?"

"Shut up. Just turn an' put your hands behind you."

"You're going to handcuff me?"

"With all these guns lyin' around, you're damn right I am."

"My arms won't reach all the way behind. I'm too . . . too heavy."

"Then I'll bust your stinkin' arms an' make them reach. Now do what I told you."

Longarm managed to cuff Jiggs's hands behind him, but it took some doing and the metal bracelets were biting deep into the fat man's flesh by the time they were done.

Jiggs did not bother complaining. By then he probably knew it would do no good.

"Fine," Longarm said. "Now let's all go for a little drive in the country, shall we?" He took the buggy whip out of the socket and popped it over the mare's ears, and they lurched into motion.

Chapter 39

The sun was out of sight, sinking behind the mountains to the west, when Longarm found a spot he liked. On the far side of a quiet brook there was a stand of shoulder-high scrub oak that covered several acres. The dense brush should stop anyone from approaching from that direction. If someone tried, their passage would be noisy indeed.

To the east was a bare, rock bluff standing twenty or thirty feet high. Tall enough to discourage nocturnal sneaking.

Which meant that Longarm had to worry only about defending from one direction. Perfect.

He drove the buggy through the creek and onto the east bank, then stopped and stepped down. The little mare had been worked hard the past two days. She deserved a rest, too.

Longarm parked the buggy with the poles pointed back toward the road, then unhitched and unharnessed. He had no grain to give the horse, but he did hobble her and let her graze on the wiry grass that grew beside the stream.

"Get down," he ordered Jiggs.

"You'll have to help me. I'll lose my balance and fall if I try to get down with my hands manacled like this."

Longarm grinned. "Then you'll fall, won't you."

"I can't—"

Longarm grabbed hold of one meaty forearm and pulled, unbalancing the big man. Jiggs toppled sideways with a shriek. He hit the rocky ground hard. Longarm could hear the breath driven out of him by the fall.

"Yeah, I thought you could get down," Longarm drawled. He nudged Jiggs in the ass with the toe of one boot and said, "Go over there. See that twisty ol' scrub oak? I want you t' set up close against it, back to the trunk."

"I can't get up and walk. I hurt myself," Jiggs complained.

"Then crawl, you cocksucker, but get your ass over there. *Now!*"

Jiggs climbed to his feet and lumbered over in the general direction Longarm had indicated.

"Right there. Now sit down."

This time, the man complied without comment. Longarm went to him and unlocked the handcuffs that had his arms pinioned behind him.

"Well, it's about time." Jiggs immediately began trying to rub some life and feeling back into his arms. "I'm hungry," he announced loudly.

"I'll feed you when we get to Buffalo."

"I am your prisoner. You are responsible for my well-being. I happen to be a lawyer, admitted to the bar in the state of Illinois. I know my rights."

"Then you'll understand if I tell you to eat shit," Longarm said.

"Speaking of which, I have to go."

"Fine. Shit in your britches for all I care. Hold your hands behind you."

"I can't—"

Longarm nudged him again, this time with the muzzles of the shotgun. Contrary to his original statement, Jiggs could. He put his hands behind him, and Longarm gave them a hard pull so he could snap the handcuffs back in place, but this time with the rough bole of an iron-tough scrub oak locked between them.

"That hurts."

"When we get to Denver, you can file a complaint with my boss. I'll make sure you have all the forms you need t' do it," Longarm said.

"You aren't very sympathetic, are you?" Jiggs moaned.

"Nope. Not the least bit, mister. Not where you're concerned."

"When my men get here—"

"If your men try an' rescue you, the first thing I'm gonna do is shoot you. That way we got nothing t' fight about. If you want t' figure out a way to tell them that, go right ahead. Now shut the fuck up a minute, will you?"

Longarm had no food or camp gear with them, but a little inventiveness generally worked wonders. He unfolded the canvas buggy top and used his knife to slice a piece off, about a foot and a half square. He folded that into a crude cone and pinched the pointed bottom closed so he could dip some water from the brook and carry it to Glenda.

He allowed a thin dribble of water to drop onto her lips. The girl did not respond.

Longarm placed his fingertips against her throat. His heart sank. "Aw, shit," he mumbled. The battered girl's body was already beginning to cool. By morning, she would have stiffened into this position.

He returned to Benito Jiggs and very slowly, very calmly explained, "Mr. Jiggs, I already have you under arrest on federal charges. But I won't object if the territory o' Wyoming decides it wants a crack at you, too."

"Charges? What charges? I told you. I am a lawyer. I know the law. I have done nothing that would violate federal law, and you have no jurisdiction when it comes to territorial law. Whatever charge you lay, I can have thrown out before nightfall."

Longarm smiled. "In Yesterday certainly. In Buffalo maybe. But we ain't going there for your arraignment, Jiggs. I'm gonna take you down to Cheyenne, where I'm the one that has friends in the courthouse. T' tell you the truth, I'm hopin' you serve your time in a federal pen first, then come back to the territory to hang."

"Hang? You are being absurd. You have no cause to even hold me here against my will," Jiggs blustered.

"You're a lawyer? Then you may 've heard o' the Fourteenth Amendment to the Constitution o' the United States."

"What the devil would that have to do with anything?" Jiggs grumbled.

"It prohibits involuntary servitude. What it actually says is that you can't deprive somebody of their life an' liberty without due process of law. The way I see it, you did exactly that when you kidnapped Glenda Bateman and—"

"Her name is Sally something-or-other," Jiggs corrected.

"I don't give a fuck what her right name was. You kidnapped her. Beat an' tortured her. Killed her. I call that violation o' the Fourteenth Amendment as far as us federals are concerned, an' murder so far as territorial law goes." Longarm paused, then added, "They're gonna need a real sturdy gallows when they swing you. Even money says your head will tear off from the drop. What d' you want t' bet?"

"Oh, Jesus. Don't . . . say things like that."

It was getting dark. Longarm eased back away from the

blubbering fat man and found himself a slight depression in the ground. He lay down and made himself as comfortable as possible. Wriggled and squirmed and tossed away all the stones and twigs that poked into his flesh.

Then he settled down to watch, out of Jiggs's sight, but where he could see as much as possible by the starlight in the night sky and where he could hear if anyone tried to approach.

It figured to be a long night.

Chapter 40

Sometime past midnight, Longarm heard the slow, soft crunch of approaching footsteps. Whoever it was was in no hurry. But then neither was he. Very carefully, he felt the action of the shotgun to verify—again—that the double gun was cocked and ready to fire. Then he spoke.

"If those boys out there start something, fat man, the first thing I do is t' fire both barrels of No. 2 lead shot into your belly. It's a big enough target. I ain't likely to miss. An' in case you're wondering can I see you in this little light now the stars are mostly clouded over, I just a minute ago seen you try and scratch yourself. But you do what you think is best, hear."

The truth was that Jiggs was sitting deep in the tangled mass of brittle scrub oak, and Longarm could not see shit. But he had heard Jiggs move a little, and assumed the man was trying to scratch one of the nagging itches that were bound to be deviling him by now.

Jiggs cleared his throat and spat, then in a loud, clear voice called, "Don't try it, Homer. You and Freddy back off now. He . . . he will shoot me if you try anything now. But don't worry. Just . . . stay close. That is all. Stay close."

159

The footsteps receded as slowly as they had come. After five minutes or so, Longarm thought he heard a horse whicker somewhere nearby.

Then there was nothing.

"What are you doing, damn you?"

"Driving, of course."

It was a good hour past sunrise and Longarm had turned off the road to Buffalo.

"Where are you going? Where are you taking me?"

"I'm taking your fat ass to prison, that's where you're going. An' I figure t' get there by way of Fort Laramie an' Cheyenne."

"I thought we were going to Buffalo," Jiggs grumbled.

"My my, is that so," Longarm responded.

He had had plenty of time to think during the night, lying there in ambush in case Homer and Freddy came. It occurred to him that Jiggs had implied that he had a tame officer of the law in Buffalo, someone who could get him out of any trouble Longarm got him into. A magistrate, perhaps, who could set bail for Jiggs, or simply a deputy who would be willing to turn a key and free the son of a bitch.

Longarm was not going to risk letting Jiggs get away with something like that.

The man had killed Glenda Bateman. He had almost certainly ordered the death of Jim Franklin.

He was not going to walk away from those crimes.

"Lemme ask you something," Longarm said late in the morning. "Marshal Franklin who was there before me. Why'd you have him gunned down?"

Jiggs thought for a moment before he spoke, perhaps assessing his chances of getting free and wanting to rub

Longarm's nose in it when he did. "That gray-haired old bastard was supposed to just give my town the illusion of law and order. Who the hell knew he would take the job seriously? When he found out what I was doing there, he threatened to call in a friend of his. Some deputy U.S. marshal who . . ." Jiggs stopped speaking. The man's eyes went wide with recognition. "You?"

Longarm nodded. "Ayuh. We was friends, Jim and me. He taught me what bein' a lawman is all about. You shouldn't ought to've had him murdered, Jiggs. That mistake is gonna cost you your life."

"I have the right to see a lawyer, you know," Jiggs said.

Longarm ignored him.

Sometime past noon, the tired mare pulled them into the stagecoach relay station on the Laramie-to-Buffalo road. She must have recognized her home barn because she picked up her speed and headed straight for it.

"A lawyer," Jiggs said stubbornly. "I demand to see a lawyer."

Longarm paid no attention to the man whatsoever.

Chapter 41

The same express company agent came out to meet the sound of approaching hoofbeats. "Oh, it's you. Back all right, I see. The rig work out all right for you?"

"Aye, it did. Tell me, friend, d'you have an icehouse here?"

"Got a springhouse over there. No stored ice, though. Whatever for would you need ice?"

"I got a body here. Been dead a while. She oughta be put on ice, but I suppose the springhouse will do. Help me unload her, will you?"

"A woman, you say?"

"Same girl who came through here on the stage a while back. She was on the coach when I got off. I met her again in Yesterday. She died hard, though. It ain't a fit sight for a man to see."

"Then maybe I'd best get my old lady to help. She takes care of any laying out to be done around here. And there's a preacher, lives only fifteen miles or so distant. He can come speak over her if you're willing."

"She ain't my woman, but I know she won't object to being prayed over."

"I'll be right back." The express agent hurried back inside, and emerged a moment later with his wife in tow. She was a large-boned woman with a flat face and ruddy complexion. Mrs. Hancock—Longarm assumed that was their name since the station was called Hancock's—took one look under Benito Jiggs's coat and clutched her throat with one hand. "What did you do to this child?"

Longarm nodded toward Jiggs. "Ask him, ma'am. He's the one that done it to her."

Mrs. Hancock stomped across the yard to where Jiggs still sat in the buggy. She stood and peered up at him for upward of a full minute. Then she reached up and snatched him off the seat.

Jiggs fell hard. Even from across the yard, Longarm could hear the breath driven out of him by the force of his fall.

The man struggled to his feet. Mrs. Hancock gave him time to rise, then she planted her feet wide and stared at him for a moment before balling her right hand into a fist and driving it practically through Jiggs's face.

Jiggs's nose was crushed and blood splattered in all directions. With his hands cuffed behind him, Jiggs could do nothing to wipe away the torrent of blood that flowed down his chin and neck and onto his shirt.

"Are you a lawman?" she demanded of Longarm.

"Yes, ma'am."

"Is this man under arrest?"

"Yes, ma'am."

"Is he going to hang?"

"Yes, ma'am."

She spat at Jiggs's feet and snapped, "Good." Then she and her husband carried Glenda's body into the spring-house, while Longarm took care of stripping the harness from the mare and rubbing her down before turning her into her home stall.

Jiggs waited quietly until they were through; then he demanded supper. "As your prisoner, you are responsible for feeding me. You haven't fed me. Not in days."

Longarm had not eaten in even longer, but he said nothing to Jiggs. To Hancock, he said, "Would it be possible for us t' get something t' eat while we wait for the next southbound?"

"Of course. There should be stew on the stove and biscuits in the oven by now."

"You're expecting the stage?" Longarm asked, glad his luck seemed to be turning for the better.

"Not for you. You said you want to go south. I'm looking for the northbound. We won't have anything coming south until sometime tomorrow."

So much for his luck turning good.

"All right then, but we'll still be needing food. I haven't et in quite a while."

"Come inside then."

Mrs. Hancock scurried around, setting two places at the table complete with bowls, spoons, and linen napkins.

Longarm led Jiggs inside and shoved him toward the table. "Set," he ordered.

Jiggs sat. Quickly. He sniffed appreciatively at the scents coming from Mrs. Hancock's stove.

Longarm sat across the table from him.

Mrs. Hancock brought a pot and ladled generous portions of steaming hot stew into the bowls in front of each man.

"Eat. Enjoy," she said.

Longarm picked up the spoon that was beside his bowl. The stew was wonderful, its flavor perhaps made the more intense because of his hunger. "This is fine, ma'am. Thank you."

"Hey!" Jiggs snarled. "I can't eat like this."

"Not hungry?"

"I can't . . . my hands are cuffed behind me, damn you. I can't eat like this."

"That's your problem. An' watch your mouth. I won't have any cussing around Miz Hancock."

"But . . . I can't . . ."

Longarm ignored him. Eventually Jiggs understood. He dropped his head down and put his face in the stew, rooting there like any hog would do. Longarm did not feel the least damned bit bad about that.

Chapter 42

"D'you have a telegraph key, Mr. Hancock? Mine is in my carpetbag, which happens t' be in a hotel room over in Yesterday."

"I think there is one here. The man who had this station before me used it."

"See if you can find it, please."

It took a while, but eventually Hancock produced a dust-covered old lineman's key with the tap-in leads attached. By then it was dark, but Longarm wanted to waste no time. He dragged Jiggs with him the quarter mile or so to the telegraph line, set Jiggs on the ground where he could keep an eye on the prisoner, and shinnied up the pole, collecting a fair number of splinters when he did so.

Working by feel, he clipped the leads onto the wire and tried the key.

EMERGENCY STOP HANCOCK STATION COMMA HOP-
KINS EXPRESS ROUTE STOP NEED ALL AVAILABLE
DEPUTIES FEDERAL AND STATE STOP NEST OF VIPERS
MUST BE CLEARED END

He signed it Long and directed it to Billy Vail, with a copy going to the Wyoming territorial police.

Done with his message, he climbed back down and brushed himself off. He would rather face a pack of outlaws with six-guns than spend any more time clinging to the top of some spindly son of a bitch of a telegraph pole.

Longarm hauled Jiggs to his feet and started back to the station. Halfway there, he heard horses coming.

The northbound had already gone through on its way to Buffalo and beyond, and there was no coach due that he knew about. Not until tomorrow, when the southbound would carry him and his prisoner down to Cheyenne.

It sounded like a good many horses, although he could not judge exactly how many there might be.

"Hold still," Longarm said. "Let's not do anything t' call attention to ourselves out here."

Jiggs stopped and took a deep breath. "Homer. Freddy. Is that you?"

"It's us, boss."

"I'm over here with this son of a bitch marshal. Now get me loose from him. I'm getting tired of this shit."

The muzzle of Longarm's Colt nestled snug behind Benito Jiggs's left ear. "Call them off, Benny, or I pull the trigger."

"You're bluffing."

The revolver was a double-action Thunderer that did not have to be cocked for each shot. But it could be.

Longarm rolled the hammer back, letting Jiggs hear the oiled mechanism click into place. "Call my bluff," he said softly.

"Boys. Boys. Wait a minute. I . . . he'll shoot me. Back off. Get me out, but back off for now."

Longarm nudged Jiggs forward. They made the rest of

the distance to the station building in lockstep. Once inside, Longarm barred the door and told Hancock, "I'm sorry to 've brought trouble on you like this, but the choice ain't mine. D'you have any long guns t' defend this place with?"

Stagecoach stations were generally equipped by the army to withstand sieges or Indian attack.

"I have a box of Springfields and a case of ammunition," Hancock said.

"Then you'd best break them out. Mrs. Hancock, I want to put you in charge of watching Jiggs here. If he gives you any trouble, whack him again like you done before. Hancock, you an' me best close and bar all the shutters. I've already sent a wire to my boss asking for help t' clean up Yesterday. Reckon we can start with this crowd of gun toughs. An' I'm sorry about all this. Truly I am."

"Don't worry about me, young man. I've been through trouble before, and I'm still standing." Hancock handed Longarm a Springfield and a box of heavy cartridges for the rifle. He chose another for himself. "I can cover the back of the house. You take the front."

"And the sides?"

Hancock shrugged.

"Right," Longarm said. "We'll do what we can."

Chapter 43

Riders came thundering out of the night, charging the station on horseback, then veering off at the last moment while firing wildly at the building until they emptied their weapons.

Bullets thumped into the solid walls, the impacts dull and heavy. Lighter sounds came when a round would manage to find a closed door or a shutter, slamming into the sawed lumber that mercifully was thick enough to stop a bullet.

The only danger was if one of the blindly fired slugs entered a firing hole left for the use of defenders.

Mrs. Hancock saw that danger and without being asked, rushed through the place blowing out the lamps so there would be no light showing where the raiders could aim at.

"How many d'you think, Hancock?" Longarm asked after a few minutes of enduring the gunfire.

"You said there was two of them chasing after Jiggs here?"

"That's right. Homer Livingston and Freddy something-or-other."

"Well, there's a helluva lot more of them out there than

that. Uh, excuse me, Martha. I didn't mean to cuss in the house."

"I forgive you, Jacob. You have cause."

"Thank you, dear."

Longarm tried to listen, but he could not get a handle on how many attackers there might be. Far more than just the two who had been following them all the way from Yesterday.

His guess—and it was only a guess—was that one of them had continued to trail behind the buggy, an easy enough task, while the other dashed back to Yesterday for reinforcements from the outlaws who enjoyed the town as a safe haven between criminal ventures.

None of them would want their little parade rained on, and if Custis Long escaped to spread the word, their reign in Yesterday was at an end regardless of what might happen to Benito Jiggs.

Longarm just wished to hell he had not placed Jacob and Martha Hancock in harm's way like this.

That feeling was reinforced when a pistol bullet sizzled through a firing port in one of the front windows. The slug clanged off Mrs. Hancock's stove and embedded itself in the wall.

Longarm ran to that port and threw two quick shots through it. That sort of shooting was not going to hit a damn thing and he knew it, but it let him blow off a little steam along with the gunpowder.

Actually, he supposed, the way things stood, the two sides could snipe at each other the whole night through without either side causing serious damage to the other.

Unless the outlaws realized they could burn the defenders out.

And they would realize it. Sooner or later, it would occur to them.

After that . . . it was just a question of whether Billy could get a relief posse together in time to lift the siege.

With a sinking feeling in his gut, Longarm realized that help from Billy Vail in Denver or the territorial police in Cheyenne was not apt to arrive in time to save living survivors of this raid. They would come. Of course they would come.

But the only thing the rescuers would find when they got here was a burned-out relay station and three or possibly four corpses.

Longarm took a deep breath. He had caused this mess. It was up to him to clean it up.

"Jacob."

"Yes, Marshal?"

"D'you have any 12-gauge shotgun shells? Something in a heavy load like duck or buckshot."

"I got a couple boxes of single-ought buckshot. Would that do?"

"Nicely, sir. Nicely."

Longarm stepped to the side of the window lest a stray bullet find him. He very carefully began checking the loads in his own trusted Colt and in the pair of revolvers he had taken from Homer and Freddy back in the casino in Yesterday.

The stubby, sawed-off shotgun he saved for last, cramming his pockets with the dark green shot shells.

Chapter 44

"Miz Hancock."

"Yes, Marshal."

"I'm gonna slip out through this door here while Jacob will do some fast shooting out the back window. Once I'm out, Miz Hancock, I want you t' bar the door. An' don't either of you open it again. Not till you know those men have gone an' it's safe for you t' come out."

"But what about you?" the work-worn woman asked.

"I'm gonna kill them, ma'am, or go down tryin'. Now you just do as I say."

"Do you know what you are doing, Marshal?"

He grinned. "Ma'am, if I knowed what I was doing, I likely wouldn't do it. Now stand by with that door, please."

Longarm tugged his Stetson firmly in place, held the shotgun chest high, and nodded. Mrs. Hancock swung the door open and Longarm, ducking low, bolted through it.

A very large, dark shape came at him in the night. A horse racing near. Without conscious thought, Longarm lifted the scattergun and tripped the rear trigger.

A sheet of flame and smoke spat out of the 12-gauge. The horse shied away at a dead run. But it left something behind. A heavy object fell to the ground with a thump and a clatter. A falling body, Longarm figured, and the gun that dropped out of the son of a bitch's hands.

He blinked rapidly, trying to recoup his night vision after the brightness of the shot-shell explosion. For a moment, he was as good as blind, but quickly began to see dim shapes again in the light that came down from the stars.

A horseman swept around from behind the station. Longarm could hear gunfire back there as Jacob Hancock exchanged shots with the attackers.

With a target he could actually see this time, Longarm palmed his Colt and fired one aimed round.

The raider shrieked and bent low in his saddle. A moment later, he spilled out of it and hit the ground hard.

The downed raider still had some fight in him. From his position on the ground, he squirmed around to face the station building and fired a pistol shot that sizzled close to Longarm's head.

"The hell with this," Longarm muttered. He emptied the second barrel of the shotgun into the outlaw's chest while the son of a bitch lay there writhing on the ground.

There was no more movement from the man after that.

Longarm stepped back closer to the wall of the station where he would be in the darkest of shadows. Working swiftly by feel, he broke open the action of the double gun, plucked the empties out and tossed them aside, then slipped fresh loads of buck into the chambers.

He snapped the gun action closed, and cocked both hammers just in time to meet another raider coming around the side of the building. The scattergun bellowed, and both rider and horse went down, dust and blood flying.

176

Longarm reloaded the fired chamber and eased around to the side of the building.

Dimly in the starlight, he could see a cluster of riders. At least five of them, he thought.

The distance was a little much for a shotgun, but . . .

Longarm braced the sawed-off against his hip, pointed it as best he could, and remembered to close his eyes just before the moment of discharge.

When he looked again, the little clutch of riders had broken up. At least one horse and two men were down on the ground, one of the men very much alive and cussing.

Longarm ducked low and continued around the relay station. When he got to the back window, he eased up beside it and in a low voice said, "We're gettin' them, Jacob. Stay ready in there."

"I will." It was Mrs. Hancock's voice.

"Are you all right?" he asked.

"We will be. Jacob was hurt, but he will be all right. Don't worry about us, Marshal. Do what you have to do."

"Yes, ma'am."

Longarm could not see the raiders now, but he kept getting glimpses of movement behind the barn. Apparently, the outlaws had withdrawn to a place of safety while they decided what to do next.

Fire would be the next logical step, Longarm figured. Surely, the raiders would come to that same conclusion.

It was up to him to stop them before that happened.

He left the relative safety of the station building and headed out across the bare, open yard. If any of the outlaws happened to be looking, they would surely spot him.

It had to be done, though. So he did it.

He cat-footed across the gravel to the barn and slipped

inside, grateful for the shadows there. Horses whickered and fidgeted as he made his way through the alley between the stalls.

At the back door, he paused, took a deep breath, then stepped out with the shotgun leading the way.

At least five men confronted him. One of the men saw him as he emerged from the barn.

"Hey!"

That was the man's final statement before he had a chance to explain himself to St. Peter.

The shotgun roared, and the scene was lighted by the muzzle flash.

Lead whistlers ripped into the group.

Longarm fired again, and men screamed.

He dropped the shotgun and palmed Homer Livingston's Colt. The .45 barked six times, and was dropped to the ground in favor of Freddy's Smith and Wesson.

Longarm emptied it, too, into the shrieking, plunging, confused mass of dying flesh, then tossed it down and slid his own good Colt into his hand.

He backed away, into the relative safety of the barn.

When he could see properly again, he once more stepped out.

He had no more targets.

Some of the outlaws had surely survived, but they were nowhere to be found now. Apparently, the whole crew had turned tail and run when they found themselves in the line of fire.

That was not what they had expected. Not what they wanted. Not what they were willing to stand up against.

Longarm retrieved the guns he had dropped, and took the time to reload each of them before making a slow, careful circle around the relay station, then another circle from farther out.

There were no more raiders. Not here there weren't.

He found three bodies of men who had been left behind by their comrades. Others—dead or wounded—might have been carried off by their friends. That was something he might never know.

It was enough for him to know that the siege was broken.

He went inside to see if there was anything he could do to help Jacob Hancock.

Chapter 45

"Are you Long?" asked the man riding at the head of half a dozen mounted men with badges pinned to their vests.

"Depends on how you mean that," Longarm said with a grin. "But t' answer your question, yes. Deputy U.S. Marshal Long."

The handsome man with the waxed mustaches leaned down from the saddle and offered his hand to shake. "I'm Lewis DuVal, Wyoming Territorial Police. Billy Vail said there was one of his boys up here needing help." DuVal looked around at the bodies laid out in the station yard. "It doesn't look to me as if you need much help here."

"Yeah, well, I kinda chased the sons o' bitches off. But I do need help. Or anyway, the territory o' Wyoming does." He explained about the situation in Yesterday where outlaws—and their money—were welcomed. "I thought maybe we oughta ride over there an' kick some ass."

"You have the ringleader here, I understand," DuVal said.

"That's him layin' over there." Longarm pointed and shook his head. "We had us one hell of a time dragging his fat ass out o' the station this morning."

"Caught in the cross fire, was he?" DuVal asked.

"Yeah. Something like that."

Considering the placement of the small-caliber bullet and the powder burns around the wound, Longarm thought it very likely that one of the Hancocks got pissed enough to put Benito Jiggs out of his misery. As an act of mercy, of course, to keep the poor fellow's head from coming off in a hanging.

Martha Hancock had been well and truly bothered by the things that were done to Glenda Bateman . . . or whatever the girl's real name was.

"Give me a minute," Longarm told DuVal.

He stepped inside to say his good-byes to the Hancocks, then walked over to the barn to retrieve what looked like the fittest of the riderless mounts that had been wandering nearby in the aftermath of the shooting. He led a tall black out of the barn, then stepped into the saddle. Whoever had owned the animal before left the stirrups a little short for Longarm's long legs. He took the time to adjust the stirrups, then nodded to DuVal.

"Let's go clean out that nest o' vipers," he said.

DuVal lifted a hand—Longarm got the impression that the territorial officer might well have held military command in the past—and motioned his band of police forward.

Longarm fell in behind.

By nightfall, he figured, Yesterday would be permanently cleared of outlaws.

And by tomorrow night, the town would be well on its way toward dying.

GIANT-SIZED ADVENTURE FROM
AVENGING ANGEL LONGARM.

BY TABOR EVANS

2006 Giant Edition:

LONGARM AND THE
OUTLAW EMPRESS

2007 Giant Edition:

LONGARM AND THE
GOLDEN EAGLE SHOOT-OUT

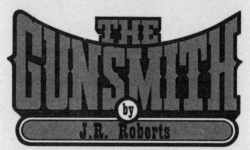

BERKLEY WESTERNS TAKE OFF LIKE A SHOT

Lyle Brandt
Peter Brandvold
Jack Ballas
J. Lee Butts
Jory Sherman
Ed Gorman
Mike Jameson

Don't miss
the best
Westerns
from
Berkley.

penguin.com

M10G0907